The Magic COOKbook

For Benjamen -
Always believe in
magic !!

Pam H. Porter

The Magic Cookbook

An Enchanting Tale Sprinkled with Recipes, Magic Charms & Fun!

Written & Illustrated by

Pam H. Porter

BALBOA
PRESS
A DIVISION OF HAY HOUSE

Balboa Press books may be ordered through booksellers or by contacting:

Balboa Press
A Division of Hay House
1663 Liberty Drive
Bloomington, IN 47403
www.balboapress.com
1 (877) 407-4847

Because of the dynamic nature of the Internet, any web addresses or links contained in this book may have changed since publication and may no longer be valid. The views expressed in this work are solely those of the author and do not necessarily reflect the views of the publisher, and the publisher hereby disclaims any responsibility for them.

This is a work of fiction. All of the characters, names, incidents, organizations, and dialogue in this novel are either the products of the author's imagination or are used fictitiously.

Certain stock imagery © Thinkstock.
Any people depicted in stock imagery provided by Thinkstock are models, and such images are being used for illustrative purposes only.

Printed in the United States of America.

ISBN: 978-1-4525-9809-3 (e)
ISBN: 978-1-4525-9808-6 (sc)
ISBN: 978-1-4525-9810-9 (hc)

Library of Congress Control Number: 2014919480

Balboa Press rev. date: 1/13/2015

For Mom, who taught me to believe,

For my family and friends, who believe in me,

For Sophie, who believed in this story,

And for my students — may you always believe in magic.

PART 1

Molly

You are often left behind,
All because you're way too kind,
In yourself you must believe,
Then great things you will achieve.

January

Molly McGregor and her two best friends ran down Main Street to Blake's Rare Books. It was the last day of their holiday break, and they all had Christmas money to spend. Molly thought it would be fun to buy something together at the brand new bookshop.

Molly, Daisy and Eva climbed the front steps of the gingerbread-colored house, opened the tall, red door and walked in.

An elderly woman holding a large gray cat approached them. "I'm Hazel Blake and this is Velvet. Welcome to our shop."

The green-eyed cat wriggled free, jumped down to the wooden floor, and dashed behind a bookshelf.

"Perhaps you should follow him," said Hazel, heading over to the cash register. "He might lead you to the perfect book."

Molly loved the idea, and she and her friends took off after the cat. But after ten minutes of circling through aisles and only occasionally catching sight of Velvet's tail as he rounded another corner, Molly stopped. "I'm getting dizzy."

Scarcely were the words out of her mouth when a book fell from a high shelf and bonked her on the head.

"Ouch!" Molly rubbed at the spot, adjusted her glasses, and then picked the book up off the floor. It had a gray velvet cover, with two green gems attached to the front. The book was worn and there was no title.

"Let's take a look at this one," said Molly and she and her friends ran to a private reading corner and plopped down on three purple chairs. Molly placed the book on the table between them and leaned over to examine it. The book glowed.

Molly gasped. "Did you see that?"

Before her friends could answer, the book flipped open to the first page.

Molly's hands flew to her face, her blue eyes opened wide. "This can't be happening."

"It's magic," said Daisy.

"But there's no such thing," said Eva.

"Then how do you explain it?" asked Daisy.

"Look," said Molly. "Words are forming on the page. It was blank a second ago."

The girls leaned in closer and Molly read aloud.

I'm filled to the brim with magical treats,
All of them cupcakes that are very sweet,
My pages are blank- that's not a mistake,
Recipes appear when you'd like to bake.

Once every month I'll come to your kitchen,
I'll teach you some tricks- if you will listen,
I'm yours for one year- but not any more,
Then I will return to this rare bookstore.

Own me together and just to be fair,
Divide up the time, so that you can share,
And one final note that's long overdue-
Always remember, the treat chooses you.

"Oh my gosh," said Molly. "It's a magic cookbook." The book snapped shut and jumped into her lap. The girls squealed with delight and sprinted to the cash register.

"Oh, how wonderful," said Hazel Blake when Molly handed her the book. "It's one of the greatest treasures in the store. You are very lucky that it found you."

"It fell on Molly's head," said Daisy.

"Well, that's a very good sign indeed," said Hazel. Before the girls could reply, she changed the subject. "Are you three ready to go back to school tomorrow?"

They all nodded. "I wish we had a few more days of vacation or even a whole week," said Molly as she tugged on her marmalade-colored braid.

"Well, you never know what this cookbook has in store for you," said Hazel, who didn't bat an eye when the book appeared to leap off the counter and into the open bag she was holding. She winked as she handed the parcel to Molly, and then crossed the room to greet another customer.

Molly adjusted her glasses on her freckled face, and glanced around the room for Velvet. She wanted to say goodbye. She noticed a cushioned bench by the window near the cash register. There were a few cat toys on it, but Velvet wasn't there. *Oh well*, thought Molly. *Hopefully I'll see him another time. He's a really cool cat.*

As Molly dashed out the door to catch up with her friends, Hazel called to her, "Let me know how it goes with the cookbook. I'm usually here in the store or upstairs in my apartment. Stop by anytime."

Molly waved and then joined Daisy and Eva next door in front of The Honeysuckle Inn. Daisy's mom owned the inn, and Daisy and her little brother lived there with her in a private wing.

"Let's go to my place," Daisy suggested.

"No, let's go to Molly's," said Eva. "She found the book, so she should have it first."

"That's okay. I can go last," said Molly.

"No," said Eva. "You should have the cookbook for the first four months, then it's Daisy's turn and then mine. It will work out perfectly."

The girls ran up Main Street and through the little town of Willow Brook. They passed the driveway to Eva's house and to her parents' flower shop, Perez Petals. Then the girls turned onto Blueberry Lane and up a dirt driveway and into the McGregors' farmhouse.

Molly led her friends down the hall and past the den where her parents and five-year-old brother Dexter were watching a movie and playing games. Daisy's brother, Arlo, was with them. He and Dexter were in kindergarten together.

As soon as the girls walked into the kitchen, The Magic Cookbook sprang out of the bag Molly was holding, nearly knocking the glasses off her face. It landed on the peach-colored countertop and then flipped open. A recipe for Coconut Blizzard Cupcakes blew onto a blank, snow-white page.

At the beginning of the recipe were the words, *Magic Cupcake Charm*, followed by a short poem.

> Coconut Cupcakes, fluffy white tops,
> Snow is falling- such big drops,
> Let's go sledding, let's go ski,
> School's called off, so we are free,
> Coconut Cupcakes, fluffy white tops,
> When they're gone, the storm will stop.

"These are so cute," said Molly, looking at the picture of the fluffy, coconut-flaked cupcakes that had appeared on the opposite page.

"Yeah, but let's look at some other recipes too," said Daisy. "You don't mind, do you Molly?"

Molly definitely *did* mind. The Coconut Blizzard Cupcakes sounded perfect. But instead she just said, "I guess not."

Daisy turned to another blank page, but immediately the book flipped back to Coconut Blizzard Cupcakes, backed away, arched its spine, and hissed. A little black storm cloud hovered above it.

"Oops. I guess I shouldn't have done that," said Daisy, her face flushing red. The book grumbled, and the cloud rumbled out tiny bursts of thunder.

"I think it's waiting for an apology," scolded Eva.

"I'm sorry," said Daisy. "I really am."

Instantly, the storm cloud evaporated, the book crept back toward them and puffed a gust of coconut-scented air into their faces.

"I think these are the ones we're supposed to make," said Molly.

After reviewing the recipe, she handed an apron to each of her friends and put one on as well. She got out mixing bowls, spoons, and ingredients, and then frowned. "We have everything but the marshmallow fluff and the coconut for the topping."

Immediately a jar of marshmallow fluff and a bag of shredded coconut appeared on the counter.

"That was incredible!" said Eva, and they began mixing ingredients together in a large bowl. Next, they lined the muffin tins with cupcake papers, spooned in the batter with an ice cream scoop, and then put the treats in the oven to bake.

When the cupcakes were cool, the girls frosted them with fluffy, marshmallow topping.

"I love this stuff," said Daisy as she piled more of it on.

"Be careful, Daisy. They're getting messy," said Eva. She slid the platter of cupcakes out of her friend's reach.

Daisy shrugged and then licked her fingers.

Worried that Eva might scold her as well, Molly was extra careful when she dipped the frosted cupcakes into a bowl of coconut flakes. Then she helped Eva top them off with miniature marshmallows.

Molly read the recipe again to make sure they hadn't forgotten anything. "Oh, here's one last thing, and it sounds really important," she said. "*When you've finished making these treats, recite the charm so that they're complete.*"

"Just like a magic spell," said Daisy. "Let's hurry up and say it."

And so they did, and when little snowflakes appeared out of thin air and sprinkled onto the cupcakes, the girls clapped.

The recipe for the Coconut Blizzard Cupcakes was still visible when the book closed. Then it drifted up onto the shelf where Mrs. McGregor kept the cookbooks for her catering business.

Molly stood on tiptoe and rifled through the books. "It's gone."

Eva looked concerned. "I hope it remembers to come back next month so that we can bake cupcakes again. After all, we have a schedule to follow."

Molly put seven cupcakes on a pretty plate and carried them into the den.

Dexter's round, freckled face beamed when he saw the cupcakes. "They look like snowballs."

"They smell yummy," said Arlo, grabbing a cupcake and stuffing it in his mouth. He got marshmallow topping on his chin, and some in his curly blond hair.

Eva rolled her eyes before handing him a napkin. "I'm so glad that I'm an only child," she muttered.

Mrs. McGregor laughed. Then she took a bite of cupcake and said, "I love coconut and marshmallow together." Everyone agreed.

Mr. McGregor adjusted his glasses. He gazed out the window overlooking the small pond behind their house. "Look. It's starting to snow. That's a surprise. This wasn't in the forecast. How very strange indeed." Frank McGregor was a scientist, and this was just the sort of thing that fascinated him. He checked the weather forecast at least twice a day.

Molly perked up. "Maybe we'll have a snow day tomorrow. I'm *really* not ready to go back to school yet."

"Keep your fingers crossed," said Daisy.

"Perhaps these really are magic cupcakes," Molly whispered to her friends, as they watched the falling snow.

* * *

It was still snowing when Mrs. McGregor woke her daughter up the next morning. "Molly, you got your wish. This is turning into a big blizzard. Schools are closed, and you have a snow day."

Molly put on her glasses, threw back her cozy quilt and ran to the bedroom window. "It looks like we already have two feet of snow." She smiled and then dashed back into her warm bed, feeling content. "Maybe I won't even leave the house today. I'll just spend the whole day at my art table."

After breakfast, while Molly was painting pictures of wintry scenes, Daisy called. "Isn't this the greatest? Let's go sledding at the park. Half the class will be there and it'll be sooo much fun! I just called Eva, and she'll meet us there."

Molly looked at the pile of paintings on her art table. They were okay, but Molly wanted to keep practicing until she was a great artist.

"I'm not sure, Daisy," said Molly. "I might just stay home and paint."

"Oh come on, Molly. Please, please, come. Please, please, please!"

Molly knew that Daisy would only keep begging, so she agreed, bundled up, and put ten cupcakes in her backpack.

"I wish I could stay here with you," Molly said to Dexter.

"And I wish I could go with you, but Daddy says the snow is too deep for me. I guess I'll just stay here and practice my magic tricks. Arlo and I have decided that we want to be magicians when we grow up."

"See you later then." Molly waved goodbye to her brother and trudged to the park with her backpack and sled.

Daisy and Eva were already there. "This is the most awesome thing ever!" said Daisy. Her frozen eyelashes and wisps of blond bangs were like miniature icicles that framed her sparkly, green eyes. Daisy's cheeks were rosy, and she had a huge smile on her face. "We haven't had a snow day in ages. I'm so glad we made those cupcakes."

Eva didn't look nearly as pleased. "It's just a giant, messy pile of snow, and I can barely see." She shivered as she wiped snowflakes off her pretty face, and pulled her red, knit hat down snugly over her ears. Her dark, frosty hair hung limply over her shoulders. "I'm freezing."

Molly stuck her tongue out and caught a snowflake. She could swear that it tasted like coconut.

Just as Daisy had predicted, lots of the other kids from their fourth grade class were there as well, climbing up the big, snowy hill and zooming down on their sleds. After their final run, Molly passed out the cupcakes. Everyone was delighted and thanked her. Despite the raging blizzard, Molly felt warm inside. She had to admit that this was just as good as painting pictures at home all day.

That night, after eating a cheesy pizza, Molly and her family watched the weather report on television. The weatherman looked worried. "This is the worst storm in recorded history, and we have no idea when it will end. Neighboring towns are experiencing warmer, clearer weather, but there seems to be a giant snow cloud over us that is not budging. Unless there's a miracle, Willow Brook schools and many businesses will be closed again tomorrow."

"I've never seen anything like this," exclaimed Mr. McGregor.

Molly watched the television for another minute, catching a close-up of Velvet the cat, sitting in the maple tree in front of Blake's Rare Books. He was batting snowflakes with his front paws. Molly tugged on her braid. *This is all so strange.*

* * *

At the park the next day, Molly, Daisy and Eva struggled to pull their sleds up the hill yet another time.

Breathless, Molly turned to Daisy as she wiped the frost from her glasses. "The snow is so deep I can hardly move. Maybe you did overdo it with the marshmallow topping."

"I told you so." Eva flashed her dark eyes at Daisy.

"Don't forget the last line of the magic cupcake charm. *When they're gone, the storm will stop,*" said Daisy.

"Then we'd better hurry back to my place and eat the rest of the cupcakes before the snow gets so deep that we can't move at all," yelled Molly through the howling wind.

By the time the girls slogged their way back to the McGregors' house, another six inches of snow had fallen, and they could barely find the front door. When Molly finally pushed it open, she tumbled into the house. Eva and Daisy fell in after her.

Dexter was sitting at the kitchen table dressed in a magician costume, finishing a cupcake with a glass of milk. "I'm bored. Mommy thought a cupcake might make me feel better."

"Great idea," said Molly. She eyed the plate in the center of the table with the remaining six cupcakes on it. "In fact, let's finish them off." She and Daisy snatched two cupcakes each and began wolfing them down. Eva picked one up and took a small bite.

"Hurry up," said Daisy. "This is not a time for good manners."

"You know, you're right," replied Eva, before she gobbled up her cupcake.

Dexter watched in awe and then grabbed the last cupcake. He ate two bites, guzzled his milk and stood up.

"Where are you going?" asked Molly.

"I'm full. I'll finish this later," Dexter explained.

"No!" Molly, Eva and Daisy all screamed at the same time. "Finish it now!"

Dumbfounded, Dexter sat back down and did as he was told. The girls watched him.

"You're making me nervous," Dexter mumbled, his mouth stuffed full of cupcake. When he'd finally eaten the last cupcake crumb, the snow suddenly stopped and the big, dark cloud that had been hovering over Willow Brook evaporated.

Molly smiled as the sun came out, and said, "I think things are going to be just fine."

Daisy and Eva sighed with relief, and Dexter burped.

Coconut Blizzard Cupcakes

Magic Cupcake Charm
Coconut Cupcakes, fluffy white tops,
Snow is falling- such big drops,
Let's go sledding, let's go ski,
School's called off, so we are free,
Coconut Cupcakes, fluffy white tops,
When they're gone, the storm will stop.

Ingredients for 24 Cupcakes

1 (3.4 ounce) package	coconut pudding mix
1 (14 ounce) can	coconut milk
1 (18.25 ounce) package	white cake mix
1 cup	vanilla yogurt
1/3 cup	vegetable oil
3	eggs
24	cupcake papers

Topping

2 (7 ounce) jars	marshmallow topping
1 (10 ounce) bag	miniature marshmallows
1 (14 ounce) bag	sweetened shredded coconut

Preparation

1. Preheat oven to 350 degrees.
2. Put the pudding mix and coconut milk in a small bowl. Mix thoroughly and set aside. In another larger bowl, combine the cake mix, yogurt, eggs and oil. Then pour the ingredients in the small bowl into the large bowl and beat until well mixed.

3. Line the muffin tins with cupcake papers and fill three-quarters full with batter. Put the cupcakes into the oven. Bake 17-20 minutes or until a toothpick comes out clean.* Set aside until cool.
4. Frost the cupcakes with marshmallow topping (take your time—it's messy), and dip the sticky tops into a bowl of shredded coconut. Put mini-marshmallows on top.

When you've finished making these treats, recite the charm so that they're complete.

Baker's Note
Bake until a toothpick comes out clean, means a toothpick stuck in the center of a cupcake comes out without any crumbs attached to it. This means the cupcakes are finished baking.

February

E veryone's so excited. What's going on?" Molly asked Daisy at
lunch recess one day.

"Tiffany Burnsley is having a Valentine's Day party at The
Willow Brook Country Club, and our whole class is invited."

"Yuck," said Molly. Tiffany was Molly's least favorite person in
the world. "I'm definitely not going."

Molly had moved to town with her family last summer and had
dreaded that first day of school. Making friends had never come
easily to her, but as soon as she took her seat in class, Tiffany Burnsley
and her sidekick, Jessica Jones, made her feel welcome. Every day at
lunch they invited her to sit with them, and every recess they asked
her to play. Molly especially liked Tiffany, and even told her about her
dream of getting her art on the cover of the newspaper one day. Molly
was sure that Tiffany really liked her too and would invite her over
for a sleepover. Molly couldn't wait to see the inside of the Burnsleys'
brick mansion that sat on top of the hill, overlooking town.

But to Molly's dismay, during the third week of school, Tiffany
and Jessica stopped talking to her. Every time Molly got close to

them, they laughed in her face and ran away. Molly was devastated. She couldn't figure out what she had done to deserve this.

One day at lunch, Molly tripped and dropped her tray. When her bowl of chocolate pudding toppled and sprayed her face, Tiffany finally spoke to her again.

"Hey carrot head," she yelled across the cafeteria. "You look much better now that your freckles are covered."

Daisy Humphrey stepped forward. "Leave her alone, Tiffany!"

"No problem," said Tiffany. "We don't want to be around her anyway. She's stuck up, and she's a bad artist. She'll never get on the cover of the newspaper, but I will!"

Before Tiffany could hurl more insults, Daisy pulled Molly away to the girls' bathroom and Eva Perez, who had been watching the whole thing, ran after them. "Tiffany loves to torture the new girls in class," Daisy explained.

"We should know," said Eva. "She did the same thing to us when we were both new in second grade. Jessica's not as bad, but she does whatever Tiffany tells her to do."

Molly burst into tears, and Daisy said, "You're not stuck up at all. You're just a bit shy." Then she added, "I would love to be your friend."

"Me too," said Eva, as she carefully washed Molly's glasses and cleaned the pudding out of her braids.

From that day forward, Molly had two new best friends.

* * *

"Guess what?" Daisy said to Molly two days before Tiffany's party. "Eva and I just found out that everyone's supposed to make a dessert for the party. There's going to be a prize for the best one."

Molly's face brightened. "Well, that changes everything. I'll definitely go. I hope The Magic Cookbook shows up again and gives us the best recipe ever. That way we can beat Tiffany."

On the afternoon of the party, the girls stood in the McGregors' kitchen and stared up at the shelf. "I sure hope it comes back," said Eva.

As if on cue, The Magic Cookbook peeked out from between the other cookbooks.

"Woo-hoo!" the girls all cried, just as the cookbook leaped and landed gracefully on Molly's shoulder where it nuzzled her neck. Then it slid down her arm, gold sparks flying everywhere, landed on the kitchen counter, and opened to another blank page.

A recipe for Heaven-Sent Cupcakes, written in scarlet, rose-scented ink slowly appeared. Once again, a magic cupcake charm introduced the recipe.

> If you want to fall in love,
> With a treat from up above,
> Here's the recipe for you,
> Filled with sticky, chocolate goo,
> Clocks are ticking—what a waste,
> Hurry up and have a taste,
> Other foods just can't compare
> To these cupcakes—oh so rare,
> You'll soon see it's evident
> That these gems are Heaven-Sent.

"My mouth is already watering," said Molly. Then she, Daisy and Eva whipped up a double batch of gooey, chocolaty cupcakes. After they pulled the heavenly treats out of the oven, they frosted them with chocolate frosting and decorated them with the chocolate heart-shaped candies that had magically appeared on the kitchen counter.

Molly reviewed the recipe. "Oh, here it is again," she said. "*When you've finished making these treats, recite the charm so that they're complete.*"

When the girls recited the magic cupcake charm, tiny gold stars appeared above the cupcakes and sparkled. Then the stars drifted over to The Magic Cookbook, which was still on the counter. A moment later, the cookbook vanished into thin air.

"Whoa!" said Daisy. "That was really impressive."

Molly smiled. "We're sure to win the dessert contest and put Tiffany in her place."

*   *   *

When Molly, Daisy and Eva arrived at the country club that night, they set their platter of cupcakes at one end of the dessert table, right next to one of the most spectacular cakes Molly had ever seen.

The tall pink cake was shaped like a castle, its glittering towers lined with silver candies. The castle was surrounded by a water-filled moat stocked with real gold fish. An enormous sugar cookie drawbridge stood at the entrance to the castle whose turrets were topped with bright red cherry candies. *Made by Tiffany Burnsley* was spelled out in shimmering silver frosting next to the moat.

A photographer from *The Willow Brook Times* was taking pictures of the glorious cake.

Molly tugged nervously at a lock of her hair, which she'd worn down tonight. She turned to her friends. "Did Tiffany really make this?"

"There's no way," said Daisy. "Someone so awful could never make something so wonderful."

"She's always bragging about Jacques, their French pastry chef. I bet he made it for her," said Eva.

"But that's not fair," Molly complained, looking at all of the other ordinary tarts, cookies and candies on the table. Their Heaven-Sent Cupcakes definitely stood out from the rest, but there was no doubt that the pink castle cake cast a shadow over everything.

Molly glanced around. The room glistened with dozens of white candles. Pink roses perfumed the air and red lanterns shaped like hearts dangled from the high ceiling. Everyone was decked out in red party clothes, just as Tiffany had instructed. It looked like a big, beautiful Valentine. Molly wished she could relax and enjoy the party, but she couldn't stop thinking about Tiffany's cake.

"Cheer up," said Daisy comfortingly. "I bet Tiffany doesn't have a magic cookbook."

"But we don't have Jacques," said Molly, immediately feeling guilty. What if The Magic Cookbook could somehow hear her?

The band on the stage played a few chords, and then a spotlight lit up the top of an ornate staircase. Molly and her friends cringed as they watched Tiffany descend the stairs wearing a pink satin dress and a pink tiara on top of her flowing brown hair.

"Of course she's not wearing red like the rest of us," whispered Eva. "She wants to stand out."

"She should've worn green to go with her toad-like personality," Daisy muttered, just before Jake Farmer, one of the fourth grade boys, yelled, "Her Majesty has arrived!"

Jake's friend, Josh Wiley, and a few of the other boys snickered.

Tiffany glared at them and then continued in a regal tone. "Welcome to my party." When she reached the bottom of the staircase, she glided around the main floor, saying hello here and there, and acting like a queen among her subjects. But to Molly's delight, no one was paying her much attention.

Tiffany marched back to the stairs, climbed the first few steps, and with a wave of her arm, signaled for the band to stop. "The judges will now taste the desserts and announce the winner," she said.

Five adults walked over to the dessert table. Each wore a red ribbon with the word *Judge* on it. Mr. Clark, their fourth grade teacher, was the head judge. He smiled at his students. "These all look delicious."

Theodore Clark was a kind, elderly man, and the students all adored him. Molly felt lucky to have him as her teacher before he retired at the end of the school year. Like Molly, Mr. Clark loved to paint. Molly couldn't wait for the painting party that he was planning for the class in April.

Mrs. Parker, the school principal, was a judge, and so was Miss Plum, the plump school librarian. Mr. Vine, the fifth grade teacher, was also a judge. He was the meanest teacher in the school, and all of the fourth graders were dreading being in his class next year. The only thing they were looking forward to was the holiday fair that the fifth graders put on for the whole school in December. Mr. Vine always chose one of his students to be in charge of the event. It was a huge honor, and Molly knew that Eva longed for the position.

Molly studied the final judge. She'd never seen the stern, stocky man before. Just like Mr. Vine, he had a sour look on his face, like he'd eaten a lemon and couldn't get the bitter taste out of his mouth.

"Who's he?" Molly asked.

"That's Tiffany's father, Mr. Burnsley," said Eva.

Molly frowned. "He looks even meaner than Tiffany."

The girls watched the judges make their way down the table,

tasting the various desserts. As Mr. Vine nibbled on a chocolate chip cookie, Miss Plum and Mrs. Parker each polished off lemon bars. Mr. Clark looked delighted with a heart-shaped strawberry muffin, and Mr. Burnsley had a few bites of an apple tart.

Then, quite unexpectedly, the castle cake's drawbridge lowered and a music box played, *Somewhere Over The Rainbow*, from somewhere inside the cake. There were faint popping sounds as tiny pink fireworks burst out of the castle towers to form little hearts. Everyone, including Molly, Daisy and Eva, oohed and aahed. It was truly enchanting.

Molly nudged her friends. "Look."

A tall man wearing an apron and a starched white chef's hat stepped forward and bowed. The name *Jacques* was embroidered in blue thread on his pocket. He sliced off the top of a cake tower, and handed it to Mr. Burnsley who gobbled it up. "Tiffany, it's delicious!"

His daughter walked over to him expectantly. "Is the contest over, Daddy?"

"Yes, sweetheart. Yours definitely takes the cake."

Molly waited for Daisy or Eva to speak up. Surely one of them would remind the judges that they hadn't tasted their cupcakes yet. But after an agonizing minute of watching Tiffany gloat, Molly realized that it was up to her.

"But there's one final treat," she said. "You still need to taste those." She pointed at the platter of Heaven-Sent Cupcakes now sitting dangerously close to the table's edge.

Molly held her breath as Mr. Burnsley slowly picked up a cupcake and took a bite. Instantly a look of pure joy spread across his face. "This is the most delicious thing I've ever tasted in my life!"

The other judges rushed over and tasted the dreamy treats.

"Absolutely incredible," said Mrs. Parker.

"These cupcakes taste like they were made in heaven," said Mr. Clark.

"They certainly do," said Mr. Vine and Miss Plum at the same time. Then they looked longingly at each other.

Molly and her friends giggled. "Maybe the cupcakes have put a love spell on them," whispered Molly.

Suddenly everyone rushed to scoop up the Heaven-Sent Cupcakes. Everyone, that is, except Tiffany Burnsley, whose face was as pink as her tiara. "But they can't possibly be better than Jacques' cake." Tiffany's face turned even pinker. "I mean *my* cake."

"Buttercup," said her father. "That cake is wonderful, but these cupcakes are better. Much, much better." He smacked his chocolate-covered lips together, declared the Heaven-Sent Cupcakes the best dessert and presented a check to Molly, Daisy and Eva.

Like an empress who had been dethroned, Tiffany threw her tiara onto the floor and stomped on it. It splintered into hundreds of pieces. "Daddy, it was your idea to have this stupid party. I didn't want to have it in the first place," she screamed.

"But, honeybunch," said her father, "I've paid for your cake to be on the cover of *The Willow Brook Times*. Aren't you happy about that?"

"I thought I'd be in the picture, too," Tiffany screamed. "I'm going home!" And with that, Tiffany stormed out of the country club, with Mr. Burnsley, Jessica Jones, and a sulky, skinny woman who Molly assumed was Mrs. Burnsley, trailing after her.

A moment later, Mr. Burnsley rushed back into the room and snatched one of the last cupcakes from the platter. "One for the road," he said to the shocked guests. As he bolted out the side door, Velvet the cat dashed in, scurried over to Molly and did figure eights through her legs, purring all the while.

Molly giggled and then bit into her cupcake. "Oh my gosh," she sighed. "This really is the best thing I've ever tasted." The cupcake was moist and rich and made her feel happy inside.

Daisy and Eva were already eating theirs and nodded.

Molly heard snippets of conversations around her.

"These cupcakes are to die for."

"I'll have to get the recipe."

"I can't stop thinking about them."

Molly smiled to herself, and then heard a voice calling out from behind her. "Oh there you are, you rascally cat."

Molly turned and saw Hazel Blake enter the room and stride towards her. Hazel leaned over and picked up Velvet who was still at Molly's feet, purring loudly.

Stroking his soft gray coat, Hazel smiled. "Nothing can beat a Heaven-Sent Cupcake. Nothing."

Then Hazel winked and carried Velvet out into the starry night.

The party raged on with music, dancing, games, and lots of laughter. Molly secretly suspected it was all the merrier because the Burnsleys weren't there. It was the best party she'd ever been to.

At the end of the evening, Jacques sliced up the mighty castle cake and passed pieces around to everyone.

"You know, this really is good," said Molly after she'd taken a big bite.

"Yes, but our cupcakes are the best," said Eva. "Molly, I'm so glad you spoke up before they decided on the winner."

"And because of you, we won," said Daisy.

Molly beamed for a moment, and then she had a very uncomfortable thought.

But we didn't win. The Magic Cookbook did.

Heaven-Sent Cupcakes

Magic Cupcake Charm
If you want to fall in love,
With a treat from up above,
Here's the recipe for you,
Filled with sticky, chocolate goo,
Clocks are ticking—what a waste,
Hurry up and have a taste,
Other foods just can't compare
To these cupcakes—oh so rare,
You'll soon see it's evident
That these gems are Heaven-Sent.

Ingredients for 24 Cupcakes

1 (3.4 ounce) package	instant chocolate pudding mix
1 & 1/3 cup	buttermilk
1 (18.25 ounce) package	devil's food cake mix
1 cup	sour cream
1/2 cup	vegetable oil
3	eggs
1 & 1/2 cup	large chocolate chips
24	cupcake papers

Topping

1 (16 ounce) tub	chocolate frosting
24	chocolate kiss candies
	cake sprinkles
	heart-shaped Valentine candy

Preparation

1. Preheat oven to 350 degrees.
2. In a small bowl combine the chocolate pudding and buttermilk. Stir and set aside. In another larger bowl, combine the cake mix, sour cream, oil and eggs. Add the pudding mixture and beat for 4 minutes at medium speed. Stir in the chocolate chips.
3. Line the muffin tins with cupcake papers and fill three-quarter's full. (These cupcakes will be bigger than most.) Put the cupcakes into the oven. Bake 19 to 23 minutes. (They should be slightly gooey.) Set aside to cool.
4. Frost the cupcakes with chocolate frosting and decorate with cake sprinkles, chocolate kisses and candies. Pile it on!

When you've finished making these treats, recite the charm so that they're complete.

Baker's Note
Use colored sprinkles over a pan or bowl. That way if some spill, you can still use them.

March

olly sat at the breakfast table with her family and took a deep breath. She leaned forward and blew out the ten birthday candles on the cinnamon coffee cake that her mom baked for her every year. It was the same one that Mrs. McGregor sold to The Honeysuckle Inn for their holiday brunches. Molly loved it.

"You and your friends should have a perfect night for skating," said Molly's father, who had just come inside from hanging strands of green clover lights around the pond in the backyard. "The ice is smooth, and it's a full moon."

Molly had been looking forward to her tenth birthday for weeks now, planning every last detail of her ice skating slumber party. She'd invited Eva and Daisy and three other girls from their class as well.

Two days before the celebration, Tiffany cornered Molly on the playground. "I overheard you talking about your party, and I'd love to come. After all, you just came to mine so it's only fair."

Before Molly could respond, Tiffany continued. "By the way, have you seen this?" She flashed the infamous cover of *The Willow Brook Times* in front of Molly's face.

Tiffany had been carrying the newspaper around with her for the past three weeks and had already shown it to Molly and everyone else in their class a zillion times.

Molly looked at the giant picture of the pink castle cake once again. The caption below it read, *Tiffany Burnsley: Local fourth grade genius*! An article followed about Tiffany and how creative she was. Molly wondered how much Mr. Burnsley had paid the newspaper to print it.

Tiffany put her hands on her hips. "And just so you know, I skate as well as I bake. You'll see for yourself when I'm at your party." Then she turned and strutted away. Molly felt sick.

It was true that Tiffany had invited her to the Valentine's Day party, but she'd invited the whole class so it wasn't really the same thing. And why would Tiffany want to come to her party in the first place? Tiffany didn't even like her. What was Molly supposed to do? How do you un-invite someone to a party that you'd never invited them to in the first place? It was all too awkward so Molly just kept quiet. She didn't even tell Daisy and Eva about the incident. After all, it was one thing to be a bit shy, but it was another to be a wimp.

Molly hoped that the problem would just go away and that Tiffany wouldn't show up.

* * *

On the afternoon of the birthday party, Molly, Daisy, and Eva were in the McGregors' kitchen. "I sure hope The Magic Cookbook comes soon," said Molly, looking through the cookbook shelf once again. "I wonder where it is. We need to bake something for tonight."

Suddenly a beautiful rainbow came soaring through the window and formed an arc across the room. Molly ran to the golden pot that had appeared on the floor where the rainbow ended. She reached inside and was overjoyed when she pulled out The Magic Cookbook.

"That was amazing," said Molly, putting the book on the counter.

The book flipped open to a blank page and then revealed a recipe for Lucky Rainbow Cupcakes. When the book began to sing the magic cupcake charm to the tune of *Happy Birthday*, the girls jumped up and down with delight.

Lucky cupcakes out of sight,
See the rainbow when you bite,
Dazzling dreams will soon delight,
If you wait until tonight.

Colored cupcakes works of art,
Brilliant blue is stellar smart,
Sunshine yellow off the chart,
Rocket red comes from the heart.

Rainbow cupcakes all aglow,
Life is good from head to toe,
When you eat them you will know,
Luck lives in the colored bow.

The girls mixed the cupcake batter, divided it into four bowls, and added food coloring.

"Put in one drop at a time," said Eva. "It's really strong, and you don't want the colors to be too dark."

"It's sort of like mixing paints," said Molly, "and I'm actually getting pretty good at that."

Molly spooned a layer of the blue batter into each cupcake liner. Daisy followed with a scoop of green, and while Eva followed with yellow, she said, "Since it's your birthday, you can do two colors." She handed Molly a spoon for the fiery red batter.

After baking the tempting treats, the girls sang the magic cupcake charm, and The Magic Cookbook turned into hundreds of rainbow-colored butterflies and then flew out the window. It was all so beautiful. Molly couldn't wait to bite into a cupcake tonight, so she could see the rainbow layers inside.

But then Molly's stomach churned. *What if Tiffany shows up at the party and ruins everything?*

✳ ✳ ✳

At five o'clock, Molly's three other invited guests arrived, and Daisy's brother, Arlo, came to spend the night with Dexter. The boys immediately rushed off to the den to eat pizza and perform their magic tricks for Mr. and Mrs. McGregor.

While the girls were in the kitchen eating their own pizza, there was a knock at the back door. Molly tugged at her braid. Maybe she could just ignore it.

There was another knock. *Please make it not be Tiffany, please make it not be Tiffany!* Molly dragged herself to the door and inched it open.

Hazel Blake was standing there holding a bouquet of rainbow-colored daffodils. Velvet stood at her feet.

Molly let out an enormous sigh of relief and said, "Hi Hazel. May I help you?"

"I heard it was your birthday. I just stopped by to give you these." Hazel handed Molly the flowers.

"That's so sweet of you," said Molly. "Thank you. They're magical."

"And Molly, remember that someday you'll discover your own hidden magic." Then Hazel winked and turned to leave.

Velvet gave Molly one long, last look with his emerald eyes and then dashed off into the night after Hazel.

Molly smelled the flowers. "They're wonderful. Are they from your parents' shop, Eva?"

"No," Eva replied. "I've never seen rainbow-colored daffodils in Perez Petals. In fact, I didn't even know they existed. Hazel must've found them someplace else."

Daisy giggled. "Maybe on another planet or something."

Molly's other guests chimed in.

"She's so mysterious," said Sasha Bell. "I just love her."

"And I love Velvet," said Beth Summers. "He's mysterious, too."

"Tiffany thinks Hazel's a witch, and Mr. Burnsley says that Blake's Rare Books is a dangerous place. My mom isn't sure we should go there anymore," said Amy Lin.

"That's silly," said Eva.

"Well, if she *is* a witch," said Daisy, "She's a really good witch." The girls all nodded.

"Happy Birthday to You," Molly's friends sang, as Eva and Daisy served everyone two Lucky Rainbow Cupcakes each, topped with the whipped cream, colored sprinkles and gold-covered chocolate coins that had appeared on the kitchen counter, when no one was looking.

Molly took a big bite. "Yum. This is delicious," she said with delight, and then looked at the beautiful rainbow layers inside the cupcake. Molly felt so happy that she forgot all about Tiffany. She smiled at her friends who were all enjoying their cupcakes.

"I feel better and better with every bite," said Eva.

"Me too," said Daisy. "Let's hurry up and go ice skating."

"I'll bring the rest of the cupcakes with us. We can nibble on them outside," said Molly, sealing the remaining cupcakes in a container.

The girls bundled up and dashed down the small hill to the pond, where they sat on a big log and laced up their skates under the light of the silvery moon.

Just after Molly slipped on her second skate, she heard a car pull into the driveway and a door slam.

Oh no. Molly gulped.

"Wait for me," a familiar voice called out. "Wait for me."

Molly felt sick. Running towards them, carrying pink, fur-lined ice skates was Tiffany Burnsley.

Daisy turned to Molly and said, "What's she doing here?"

"You didn't invite her, did you?" Eva whispered.

"It's a long story," Molly mumbled, watching Tiffany sit down on the log right next to the container of remaining cupcakes. Tiffany lifted the lid and peered in.

"Hmm. I'll try one of these after I show you my new trick." Tiffany laced up her skates and glided to the middle of the pond. She skated backwards in a big circle and came to a stop. "I bet none of you can do that," she said, skating off the ice and sitting back down on the log.

Molly watched in dismay as Tiffany snatched a cupcake out of the container and brought it to her lips. But before Tiffany could take a bite, Daisy jumped up, skated onto the ice and said, "Actually Tiffany, I bet I can do that trick and one that's even better."

Daisy turned and skated backwards just like Tiffany, but then she gained speed, leaped into the air, twirled twice, and landed perfectly on one foot. Daisy looked more surprised than anyone.

Everyone but Tiffany cheered.

"How did you do that?" Tiffany stood up and screamed. "It's not fair." Then she slammed her uneaten cupcake down onto the ice where it broke apart.

"She sure loves to smash things. First the tiara, now the cupcake," Eva whispered to Molly as they watched the cupcake crumbs skid across the pond, rainbow-colored stars trailing behind them.

"What's in those cupcakes?" Tiffany demanded.

"Oh, nothing special," said Eva as she scurried onto the ice and then spun around so fast that she actually rose into the air like a tornado. A few moments later, she landed and came to a sudden stop.

One after another Molly's friends took turns performing leaps, splits and spins, while Tiffany sat on the log at the edge of the pond, looking too shocked to speak or smash anything else.

"Now it's the birthday girl's turn," said Daisy.

And everyone, except for Tiffany of course, clapped their hands and chanted, "Mol-ly, Mol-ly, Mol-ly."

Molly gulped. There was no way she could do tricks as good as her friends. She was sure she couldn't even outdo Tiffany's plain little trick. Or could she? Molly remembered what Hazel had said. *Someday you'll discover your own hidden magic.* And suddenly Molly knew that *someday* had arrived.

Molly skated to the center of the ice, adjusted her glasses and then spread her arms like a swan. She felt herself being lifted by a gentle, invisible force. As she leaped from one end of the pond to the other, a trail of colored light streamed behind her, forming a perfect rainbow over everyone below. She felt like she was painting the sky. The glow of the full moon shone through the rainbow and reflected bands of color onto the frozen pond.

Tiffany's face turned as white as snow. "I'm getting out of here! You're all witches- just like Hazel Blake." She grabbed her boots and hobbled back up the little hill to the McGregors' driveway with her skates still on. Before she flung herself into the back of her waiting limousine, she yelled up to Molly who was now sitting on top of the rainbow in the sky, "You might skate better than me, but I got on the cover of the newspaper, and you never will."

"You know Tiffany," Molly yelled back, "I could care less. There's more to being creative than getting on the cover of a silly newspaper. That really isn't what doing art is all about."

Molly didn't notice that after these words poured out of her mouth, the rainbow glowed even brighter.

Nor did she notice that Velvet was peering up at her from the roof of the McGregors' farmhouse, purring.

Lucky Rainbow Cupcakes

Magic Cupcake Charm
Lucky cupcakes out of sight,
See the rainbow when you bite,
Dazzling dreams will soon delight,
If you wait until tonight.

Colored cupcakes works of art,
Brilliant blue is stellar smart,
Sunshine yellow off the chart,
Rocket red comes from the heart.

Rainbow cupcakes all aglow,
Life is good from head to toe,
When you eat them you will know,
Luck lives in the colored bow.

Ingredients for 16 or More Cupcakes

1 (18.25 ounce) box	white cake mix
3	eggs
1 cup	water
1/3 cup	vegetable oil
	blue, green, yellow and red food coloring
16 or more	foil cupcake liners

Topping

1 can	whipped cream
16 or more	gold covered chocolate coins
	multi-colored cake sprinkles

Preparation

1. Preheat oven to 350 degrees.
2. In a medium size bowl, combine the cake mix, eggs, water and oil. Beat for 4 minutes at medium speed. Divide the batter evenly into four cups. Add drops of food coloring to each bowl to make red, green, blue and yellow. Add more drops until you get the desired shades of color. Stir well to combine.
3. Line the muffin tins with foil cupcake liners. Spoon a thin layer of blue batter on the bottom of each cup, followed by some green, then a yellow layer, and red on top. Each cupcake liner should be three-quarters full. Put the cupcakes in the oven and bake 15 to 20 minutes. Be careful not to overbake them. Set aside to cool. Make a few more cupcakes if you have extra batter.
4. When they are cool, carefully peel the foil liners off of the cupcakes. Put a dollop of whipped cream, some cake sprinkles and a gold covered chocolate coin on the top of each cupcake when ready to serve.

When you've finished making these treats, recite the charm so that they're complete.

Baker's Note

Foil cupcake liners are preferred over paper ones if you plan to peel them off before serving the cupcakes.

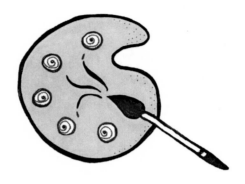

April

"'m so excited that the painting party is tomorrow," said Molly as she and her friends stood in the McGregors' kitchen one spring afternoon.

Eva turned to Daisy, "Your mom was so nice to invite us to have the party at The Honeysuckle Inn. It'll be so much better than having it at school."

"She loves having parties there," said Daisy.

"Let's make cupcakes for everyone," said Molly. She reached up to the shelf above the counter. "Maybe our cookbook is back up here this time."

She giggled when The Magic Cookbook leaned out from between her mother's cookbooks, rubbed up against her hand and then tiptoed down her arm and onto the counter.

"That was easy," said Molly. "Since this is my fourth and final turn, today's recipe is bound to be the best one yet."

Molly stroked the cover of the book, and it opened to a blank page. The girls watched as a recipe for Hidden Magic Cupcakes appeared.

I'm here to remind you– it's good to be bold,
And sometimes it's best to ignore what you're told,
To live a dull life is really quite tragic,
Be true to yourself and find hidden magic.

Molly adjusted her glasses as she looked at the picture of the cupcakes that had appeared on the opposite page. She frowned. "They just have white frosting on them and nothing else."

"How disappointing," said Eva.

Daisy scanned the recipe. "These sound really weird."

1/2 jar of pickle juice
1 can of beans
5 gray cat hairs
2 cups of dirt
3 drops of dandelion milk

Molly didn't know whether to laugh or cry. "Is this a joke?"

Daisy laughed. "It has to be."

Eva turned to Daisy. "Go ahead and flip through the cookbook for a better recipe."

"I don't know," said Daisy. "My turn with The Magic Cookbook starts next month. What if I make it mad again, and it refuses to come to my place?"

"Maybe I should try," said Molly, but as she reached out to turn to a new page, the cookbook vanished.

"Oh no," said Molly. "That was my final turn. Maybe we should've made the recipe that we were told to make. What are we going to do now?"

Daisy frowned. "I guess we're not making cupcakes for the painting party."

* * *

Molly tossed and turned in her bed that night as the Hidden Magic Cupcake charm played over and over in her head.

I'm here to remind you- it's good to be bold,
And sometimes it's best to ignore what you're told,
To live a dull life is really quite tragic,
Be true to yourself and find hidden magic.

At midnight, Molly bolted upright. "Oh my gosh," she whispered. "It's up to me to make the cupcakes. I can't believe that I didn't think of this before." She paused. "But can I really do it without The Magic Cookbook's help?"

Molly jumped out of bed, threw on her lavender bathrobe and fuzzy orange slippers, and tiptoed quietly downstairs to the kitchen.

* * *

The next day, Molly arrived at The Honeysuckle Inn a few minutes before the party. She joined Daisy and Eva who were on the back patio setting up pitchers of lemonade and plates of cookies.

"What do you have with you, Molly?" asked Eva.

"Take a look," said Molly. She put the white box she'd been carrying onto the table, next to some purple lilacs from Perez Petals.

Daisy took off the lid. "Oh wow. These cupcakes are incredible."

"Did you buy them?" asked Eva.

"Nope," said Molly. "I made them myself in the middle of the night. I realized that baking really isn't that hard. I found a recipe for Oreo cupcakes in one of my mom's cookbooks and then went wild decorating them. It was just like painting."

Daisy and Eva examined the pink frosted cupcakes that were

covered with turquoise swirls, orange dots, blue stars, yellow zigzags, red hearts and colorful, edible confetti. A paintbrush sat across the top of each cupcake.

"The paintbrushes are a nice touch," said Eva.

"After I made the cupcakes, they appeared on the counter," said Molly.

"I wonder if they're magic," said Daisy.

"I guess we'll find out soon enough," said Molly as her classmates streamed out to the patio and over to the refreshments.

"These are awesome," said Jake Farmer, grabbing a cupcake.

"Molly made them," Daisy announced.

Tiffany strutted over to the cupcakes. "These are okay but not as spectacular as my castle cake. But keep practicing, Molly. Maybe someday you'll be as creative as me, and you'll finally get on the cover of *something*."

"I can only hope so, Tiffany," Molly said in her very sweetest voice. Tiffany stood there for a moment with a confused look on her face and then walked away. Daisy giggled.

"Way to go, Molly!" said Eva.

The fourth graders carried their cupcakes to their seats at the round tables that were scattered around the patio. Each table was set up with paper and painting supplies. Molly sat between Eva and Daisy.

"Welcome class. I have a special announcement to make," said Mr. Clark. "As many of you know, since I'm retiring this year I was chosen to be the head of the school yearbook committee. What you don't know is that I'll be choosing one of your paintings today to be on the cover of the yearbook. To celebrate our school's 50th anniversary, the cover will be in color for the very first time. Needless to say, this is a big deal."

The children buzzed with excitement.

"Can we paint anything we want?" asked Amy Lin.

"It should have something to do with school," Mr. Clark replied. "But have fun with it and don't worry about making a mistake. I'm not looking for perfection."

"Can we use these?" Jake Farmer held up the paintbrush from the top of the cupcake he'd just eaten.

"Definitely," said Mr. Clark. Then he set up his own painting easel. "I'll be painting up here if you need me."

Molly's classmates dipped their new paintbrushes into the paints, and everyone got to work.

*   *   *

An hour later, Mr. Clark said, "I've never seen you all so engrossed in a project. Excellent job. Now sign your work, and let's stroll around and see the masterpieces you've created."

Molly looked at her painting of the school building. It was a little bit lopsided, but she loved the way she'd painted the green and orange ivy dancing up the sides. For fun, she'd painted a gray cat that looked like Velvet, sitting on the front steps with a happy expression on his face. A dazzling rainbow arched above the school, and bright blue dragonflies scattered the sky.

This is my favorite painting ever, thought Molly. Then she stood up, pushed in her chair and glanced down at Daisy's painting. Molly's mouth fell open. She grabbed Daisy's sleeve. "This is incredible. It looks like a photograph." Molly admired the painting of Daisy jumping on her trampoline with a bunch of adorable puppies.

Daisy said in a hushed tone, "These paintbrushes are definitely magic. All I did was hold it, and it did all of the work. It was so much fun."

Eva chimed in, "But it's such a shame that the paintbrushes lose their magic after they paint one picture. I tried to paint a second one, but it wouldn't work. Anyway, here's my first painting."

Molly couldn't believe her eyes. It was a picture of Eva at a Christmas party making a speech to everyone in their class. Every single detail was perfect.

"I can't wait to be chosen to organize the holiday fair in fifth grade," said Eva. "Painting this picture has made me even more excited about it."

"And I'm more excited than ever about getting a puppy someday," said Daisy.

Molly wandered from table to table, gawking at the lifelike paintings of the school's soccer team, the fifth grade graduation, and of the national spelling bee competition.

When Molly looked at Tiffany's beautiful painting of a girl in a tiara smiling at her perfect report card, her stomach churned. *My painting isn't good enough. Why did I make the building so lopsided? I should've been more careful. What was I thinking?*

When everyone had returned to their seats, Mr. Clark cleared his throat. "Your paintings are amazing," he said, looking more perplexed than pleased. "I had no idea that you were quite this talented." All of the children, except for Molly, beamed.

"However," he continued, "there's one painting that stands out from the rest."

All of the fourth graders held their breath.

Mr. Clark looked directly at Molly. "Molly McGregor, I love your painting. It's colorful, fun and quite delightful." Molly thought her ears were playing tricks on her. How could her painting stand out from all of the others that looked so perfect? It wasn't nearly as good.

"You heard me right, Molly," said Mr. Clark, as if he could read her thoughts. "I love it because it's not perfect and because you have your own unique style. You should be very proud of yourself. This is the painting that I'm choosing for the cover of our special yearbook. Let's all give Molly a round of applause."

As children clapped and cheered, Molly tugged at her braid and blushed. She glanced across the patio. Tiffany wasn't clapping, and she looked like she was about to cry. Molly actually felt a little sorry for her.

"Your painting really is special," said Eva.

Daisy leaned over and whispered, "Your paintbrush must've been especially magic."

Molly grinned at them both and said, "I didn't use one of *those* paintbrushes."

Eva and Daisy glanced at the Hidden Magic Cupcake that was still sitting on Molly's napkin next to her. The paintbrush lay on top, completely untouched.

"You mean, you did this all on your own?" they both asked at the same time.

"Yep. That was all me." Molly grinned, and then ate her cupcake, slipping the magic paintbrush into her shirt pocket.

*　*　*

After the party, the girls ran next door to Blake's Rare Books.

Hazel waved to them from across the room, where she was sorting through a pile of books. Velvet was sitting on his window-seat cushion. When he spotted the girls, he stood, stretched, hopped onto the floor, and sauntered over to greet them. The girls stroked his soft fur. He purred and then went back to his cushion.

"So Molly," said Hazel, walking over. "How are things going?"

"Everything has turned out better than I could've imagined," said Molly. "My art is going to be on the cover of the yearbook, and I can even stand up to Tiffany."

Hazel smiled. "I told you that someday you'd discover your own hidden magic. Well done." Hazel gave Molly a hug and then crossed the room to help a customer.

Molly felt something poking her. She reached into her shirt pocket and pulled it out. It was her magic paintbrush. "I forgot all about this."

"You'll have to paint a picture with it later," said Eva.

Molly thought for a moment. "You know, I don't need it," she said. "I love my paintings just the way they are." Then she tossed the paintbrush into the air, and it vanished.

Hidden Magic Cupcakes

Magic Cupcake Charm
I'm here to remind you– it's good to be bold,
And sometimes it's best to ignore what you're told,
To live a dull life is really quite tragic,
Be true to yourself and find hidden magic.

Ingredients for 24 Cupcakes

1 (18 ounce) package	white cake mix
1 package	Double Stuf Oreos
3	eggs
1 cup	water
1/3 cup	vegetable oil
1	large Ziploc bag
24	foil cupcake liners

Topping

2 (16 ounce) tubs	cream cheese frosting
	blue, green, yellow and red food coloring
	cake sprinkles
24	small inexpensive paintbrushes
	resealable sandwich bags

Preparation

1. Preheat oven to 350 degrees.
2. Prepare the cake mix according to package directions. Line muffin tins with foil cupcake liners. Twist apart 24 Double Stuf Oreos. Place a wafer with filling in it (filling side up) in the bottom of each cupcake liner. Place the remaining Oreos into a Ziploc bag and roll with

a rolling pin so cookies are crushed. Stir cookie crumbs into cake batter. Fill cupcake liners three-quarters full with batter. Put the cupcakes in the oven and bake 17 to 20 minutes. Set aside to cool.

3. Add food coloring to the frosting and make up a nice palette of colors to work with.

4. Put some of the colored frosting into resealable sandwich bags. Snip off a corner of each bag so that you can squeeze frosting out for decorating. Frost and decorate cupcakes any way you like. Place a paintbrush on the top of each one. Have fun!

When you've finished making these treats, recite the charm so that they're complete.

Baker's Note

For this recipe, foil cupcake liners work better than paper ones. They keep the Oreos in the batter from burning in the oven.

PART 2

Daisy

We all know that you're first rate,
But you need to concentrate,
When you feel yourself adrift,
Take your time—the fog will lift.

May

I just saw Hazel put a *Going Out of Business* sign in her store window," Molly exclaimed, as she rushed into the kitchen at The Honeysuckle Inn.

Daisy gasped. "Are you serious?"

"I know all about it," said Eva, who had already arrived for Daisy's sleepover and was sitting at the counter. "When my mom was delivering flowers there yesterday, Hazel told her that someone started a rumor that she's a witch and that Blake's Rare Books is a dangerous place."

"Tiffany Burnsley strikes again," said Molly. "I thought she was just mean to the kids in our fourth grade class. Now she's being mean to Hazel, too."

"She really is a toad disguised as a princess," said Daisy. "This is awful."

"But why is Hazel closing her store just because there's a silly rumor going around?" asked Molly, sitting down on a stool next to Eva.

"I guess customers have been staying away," Eva answered.

"That's not true. I was just over there today," said Daisy. "I got a book from the give-away bin called, *How to Raise a Puppy*."

"But you don't have a puppy," said Eva. "Whenever you ask your mom for one, she always turns you down."

"I know, I know," said Daisy. "She says I have to learn to be more responsible first."

"You mean you have to clean up after yourself?" asked Eva.

"Well, that's part of it." Daisy took a sip of milk and wiped her mouth on the sleeve of her shirt. "She says I also have to take pride in my work, I need to help out more, and I need to slow down and pay attention."

"You can do all those things, Daisy," said Molly.

"I guess so, but it would be so much easier if my mom would just go ahead and let me get a puppy now."

Coincidentally, Mrs. Humphrey popped her head into the kitchen right at that moment. "The guests are all out for the afternoon. I'm going to drop Arlo off at Dexter's, so they can practice their magic tricks together. After that, I'll run some errands. Will you girls be okay on your own for a couple of hours?"

"Don't worry Mom, we'll be fine." As Daisy stepped towards her mother to kiss her goodbye, she stumbled on her untied shoelaces.

Mrs. Humphrey frowned. "Pay attention Daisy. You're going to hurt yourself." Daisy stooped down and tied her shoelaces.

Her mother shook her head and ruffled Daisy's hair. "You girls call me if you need anything." The kitchen door swung shut behind her.

"Come on, Daisy. Show us your new book," said Molly.

Daisy reached into the purple bag and put the book on the counter. Of course she was expecting to see the book with a picture of a sheepdog puppy on the cover, but instead, the cover was gray velvet with two green gems attached.

The girls cheered. "It's The Magic Cookbook!"

"I thought you said it was a puppy book," said Eva.

"It was," said Daisy. "I even saw Hazel put it in the bag."

"Well, I guess you never know how The Magic Cookbook is going to sneak up on you," said Molly. As she stroked the cover of the cookbook, it leaned into her hand. Molly smiled and said to it, "I'm so happy to see you again. I wish I could show you all of the paintings I've done in the last month. I'm having so much fun. Thank you for all of your help."

Daisy combed her fingers through her short blond curls. *The cookbook really helped Molly, so of course it will do the same for me, too.* She looked at her friends, her eyes wide with excitement. "Maybe The Magic Cookbook will help me get a puppy!"

Before anyone could say anything else, the cookbook flipped open to a blank page, and a poem gradually appeared.

Another season of magic begins,
A new girl's in charge—but everyone wins,
You'll want to bake for hours and hours,
While you unleash your magical powers.

Baking is easy- there's nothing to fear,
I'm here to make it all perfectly clear,
And I'll remind you of what you will need,
To live a sweet life- and that's guaranteed.

As the time passes- you'll change quite a lot,
Your head will be filled with much food for thought,
So roll up your sleeves—get ready to make,
One batch per month of enchanting cupcakes.

"I can't wait to get started," said Daisy.

"And it's so wonderful that we get to bake the cupcakes here this time," said Eva.

"Daisy, you're so lucky that your mom owns this beautiful inn." Molly gazed around the impressive kitchen. Big black and white marble tiles checkered the floor, shiny copper pots hung from a fancy iron rack, and white cupboards with Italian glass knobs circled the room. A large window looked out onto the blossoming cherry trees that surrounded the back patio and Daisy and Arlo's trampoline.

"Yeah, I love living here, but it'd be even better with a puppy," said Daisy. "And, if Blake's Rare Books isn't next door anymore, it won't be nearly as much fun."

"If Hazel is a witch, why doesn't she just cast a spell that brings customers to her store?" asked Eva.

"Maybe she's not a witch. Maybe Velvet's the magic one," said Molly.

"Maybe The Magic Cookbook can help us out," said Daisy.

Scarcely were the words out of her mouth, when the cookbook turned to a new blank page, and a recipe for Goofy Golf Cupcakes rolled onto it. A magic cupcake charm introduced the recipe.

First you make these cupcakes, then later on tonight,
Place them on the bookstore lawn and come back when it's light,
What you'll find in front of you will hit you with some force,
The treats will have turned into a miniature golf course.
There's a sign that's hanging high for everyone to see—
'Buy a book from Hazel—play a round of golf for free!'
Over time and more than once this course could save the day,
But only if you're listening to what I have to say.

"I'll start mixing everything together," said Daisy.

"We'll help you," said Molly.

"No, I'll get everything ready. If I'm ever going to get a puppy, I've got to be more responsible. You two just relax." Daisy scurried around the kitchen, flinging open cupboard doors in search of bowls, measuring cups, spoons, and ingredients.

"I wouldn't exactly call this relaxing," said Eva.

When Daisy began dropping things on the floor, and saying things like, *"I can't remember if I added the eggs yet or not,"* Eva jumped off her stool.

"I can't stand it any longer," she said, grabbing a wet sponge and cleaning up after her friend.

When a bag of round lollipops, and a tube of green decorator's gel suddenly appeared from out of nowhere, Daisy clapped her hands. "I love it when that happens!"

After the pistachio cupcakes were baked and cooled, Molly turned to Daisy, "Now it's your turn to relax."

Daisy watched while Molly frosted the cupcakes with green frosting, and Eva dipped lollipops in a bowl of water to make them sticky. Next, Eva rolled them in powdered sugar until they were covered. Then she handed the lollipops to Daisy, who stuck one into the top of each cupcake.

"They look like golf balls sitting on golf tees," observed Molly. "That's so cool."

Daisy wiped her dirty hands on her jeans.

"Daisy," said Eva. "Remember, part of being responsible is cleaning up after yourself."

"You're right," Daisy replied and walked over to the kitchen sink and washed her hands.

After the girls recited the magic cupcake charm, The Magic Cookbook snapped shut, shot to the end of the counter, and then disappeared into the wall. *Poof!*

"Awesome," said Daisy. "I can't wait to see it next month."

That night, after everyone else at the inn was asleep, Daisy and her friends snuck over to the far side of Blake's Rare Books and began placing the twenty-four cupcakes around the large lawn.

Molly pointed at the bookstore where Velvet was sitting on his window seat cushion. "He's watching us." The girls could make out two green eyes blinking at them through the darkness.

Daisy waved to Velvet and then put her finger to her lips. "Shhhh, we're going to surprise Hazel."

Velvet's glowing eyes bobbed up and down, as if he were nodding.

*   *   *

The next morning the girls wolfed down their cereal and orange juice and ran next door to the bookstore lawn. Just as the magic charm promised, they were dumbstruck by what they saw. The cupcakes had been replaced by the most magical miniature golf course any of them could possibly imagine.

There were twenty-four miniature models of real places around the world: the Eiffel Tower, London Bridge, some Dutch windmills, the Sahara Desert, the Amazon Rainforest, a Hawaiian volcano, the Grand Canyon and many others. Daisy especially loved all of the water features. Her very favorite was a little replica of Niagara Falls that spilled into a churning pool, full of little waves that tossed and turned and even created mist that sprayed the girls.

Each model had a series of paths for the golf balls to wind through. At Niagara Falls, you had to hit the ball into a little barrel, which would then roll down the waterfall and splash into the pool below. When the barrel floated to the shore, you hit the ball into another barrel before moving on to Las Vegas, the next hole.

At the entrance to the course, there were tubs of golf clubs, colored balls, pencils and score pads. There was a tall sign that said, *Buy a Book From Hazel, Play a Round of Golf For Free*! And below that sign was a smaller one, *Open Until The End of Summer.*

Hazel unlocked the front door of the bookstore and walked out to the side lawn, Velvet close at her heels. Tears came to her eyes as she surveyed the enchanted scene. "This is just wonderful."

A few minutes later, a group of children gathered, staring wide-eyed at the golf course.

Hazel smiled. "Looks like it's going to be a busy day. I could sure use some help inside."

Molly and Eva ran into the store.

"And Daisy," Hazel called from the porch, "let us know if you need help out here."

"I'll be fine on my own. This is going to be easy." Daisy picked up a golf club and hit a ball onto the tiny raft in the tiny Colorado River in the Grand Canyon. Almost immediately, the raft tipped over, and the ball shot into the air. Then it sailed across the lawn, bounced onto the sidewalk and made its way down Main Street. Daisy chased after it.

When she returned with the ball ten minutes later, children had already come out of the bookstore with their new books and were playing miniature golf.

"This is the greatest golf course anywhere," said Jake Farmer.

"You're so lucky you get to help here, Daisy," said Sasha Bell.

Dexter was there and waved. "My mom's next door drinking coffee with your mom."

"They gave us enough money for two books each, so we can

play twice," yelled Arlo from Niagara Falls. "We got books about magicians."

Daisy felt someone tugging on her baggy shirt. "I lost my ball in the Sahara Desert," sobbed a little girl with blond pigtails.

"The lava in the Hawaiian volcano got clogged, and it's not working right," cried another little girl.

"Niagara Falls is out of control, and I'm soaking wet," Arlo yelled. "Help me Daisy."

"The little bear escaped from the Alaskan Wilderness and is climbing the Eiffel Tower," yelled Dexter.

"What a surprise. The golf course is breaking down already," snarled a girl from the sidewalk. "It's probably haunted, just like the bookstore."

Daisy turned around. *Oh great. What's she doing here?* Daisy put her hands on her hips and yelled, "If you really feel that way Tiffany, then why don't you leave?"

"Gladly." Tiffany marched away, her long brown ponytail swinging behind her.

Daisy scowled after her and then handed the little girl with pigtails a blue golf ball.

"But I don't want this one. I want my pink one that's buried over there in the Sahara Desert," she cried.

Daisy followed the girl and then stuck her hands into the sand. After two minutes of digging, she presented the pink ball to the girl.

Then Daisy wandered to the next hole and shoved the end of a golf club down inside the Hawaiian volcano. Warm lava sputtered and spewed until the volcano was unclogged.

This is sort of fun, thought Daisy. *I like fixing things.* She looked carefully at Niagara Falls. *Hmm. I wonder why they're flowing backwards? I wonder what will happen if I turn this?* Daisy fiddled with a knob until, much to her delight, Niagara Falls started flowing the right direction. "There," she said to her wet brother.

"Thanks a lot, Daisy." Arlo beamed at his sister. "Mommy would be proud of you."

Daisy patted Arlo on the back and then strode over to the Eiffel Tower. She snatched the tiny bear off the structure and carried him back to the river in the Alaskan Wilderness. Then she scooped up a tiny salmon that was swimming upstream and dangled it in front of the bear's nose. He sniffed it for a second and then swallowed it down whole. Then he began catching fish on his own.

Dexter jumped up and down. "That was awesome. I don't think he's going anywhere now."

Forty minutes later, Daisy had gotten all of the kinks out. The golf course was running smoothly. Children continued to stream through, and Daisy was delighted to see a few adults as well. When Mr. Vine and Miss Plum went through the course holding hands, Daisy stared. *I wonder if they're really in love or if they're still under the spell of the Heaven-Sent Cupcakes.*

Molly and Eva ran out of the bookstore. "We would've come sooner, but it was a mob scene inside. You're so lucky that you just got to hang out here and have fun."

Daisy laughed. "Yeah, it's been a piece of cake."

*　*　*

At twilight, Hazel said goodbye to her last customer of the day and locked up the bookstore. Before she took the girls out for a "thank you dinner" at The Hilltop Soda Shop, they stood in the lawn, admiring the enchanted golf course.

"It was a great day," sighed Daisy.

"It certainly was," Hazel replied.

"I guess this means you don't have to close the store," said Molly.

"Not if I still have customers," said Hazel. "And not if Daisy stops by from time to time to make sure the golf course is running smoothly."

"I'd be happy to," said Daisy and then leaned over to tie her shoelaces.

When Hazel, Eva, and Molly started walking up the street, Daisy yelled, "I'll catch up with you guys in a minute."

Daisy glanced back at the bookstore lawn. Velvet was running circles around the golf course, pink and yellow sparks flying from his fur.

That is one mysterious cat, thought Daisy and then skipped up the street to join her friends.

Goofy Golf Cupcakes

Magic Cupcake Charm
First you make these cupcakes, then later on tonight,
Place them on the bookstore lawn and come back when it's light,
What you'll find in front of you will hit you with some force,
The treats will have turned into a miniature golf course.
There's a sign that's hanging high for everyone to see—
'Buy a book from Hazel—play a round of golf for free!'
Over time and more than once this course could save the day,
But only if you're listening to what I have to say.

Ingredients for 24 Cupcakes

1 (3.4 ounce) package	pistachio instant pudding
1 & 1/4 cup	milk
1 (18.25 ounce) package	yellow cake mix
1/3 cup	vegetable oil
3	eggs
24	cupcake papers

Topping

1 (16 ounce) tub	white frosting
	green food coloring
	green decorator's gel
	green decorator's sprinkles (optional)
24	lollipops (the kind with round ball candies and straight white sticks)
1 cup	powdered sugar

Preparation

1. Preheat oven to 350 degrees.
2. In a small bowl combine the pistachio pudding and milk. Stir and set aside. In another, larger bowl, combine the cake mix, oil and eggs. Add

the pudding mixture and beat for 4 minutes at medium speed. Add a few drops of green food coloring to the batter and stir.

3. Line the muffin tins with cupcake papers and fill them three-quarters full with batter. Put the cupcakes in the oven. Bake 17 to 20 minutes. Set aside to cool.

4. Color the frosting green and use it to frost the cupcakes. Squeeze on a few lines of green decorator's gel for blades of grass. Unwrap the lollipops, dip the candy ends in a bowl of water and then dip them in a bowl of powdered sugar. Then stick one into the center of each cupcake (stick first). These are the golf balls on golf tees. If you like, sprinkle cupcakes with green decorator's sprinkles.

When you've finished making these treats, recite the charm so that they're complete.

June

"I'm so glad school's out for the summer," said Daisy one evening. The Honeysuckle Inn was closed for the night, and Daisy's mom and brother were out of town until tomorrow afternoon. Daisy had invited Molly and Eva over, and Hazel was staying with them. She was already upstairs in one of the guest rooms reading.

"I'm glad it's summer, too," said Molly, "It means that Tiffany's away at her beach house, and we don't have to see her for at least two months."

"And we don't have to hear her telling everyone that the miniature golf course is haunted," said Eva.

"Well, no one's listening to Tiffany," said Daisy. "Hazel's store is booming, and everyone loves the golf course."

Molly sighed. "I won't miss Tiffany, but I'm really going to miss Mr. Clark. He's the best teacher ever. Too bad he just retired."

"I'm not looking forward to having mean Mr. Vine for fifth grade," said Eva. "But I am looking forward to the holiday fair. I can't wait to be chosen to organize it."

"Well," said Daisy. "Let's not think about any of that right now. Let's do something fun."

Suddenly, The Magic Cookbook burst out of a kitchen cupboard, leaped onto the counter, cracked open an inch, and began panting like a dog. When the book flew open to a blank page, slobber flew everywhere, and a recipe for Pupcakes appeared, along with a magic cupcake charm.

Little pupcakes everywhere,
Treats like these are very rare,
In the morning you'll have found
They've turned into special hounds,
One by one they'll disappear
Straight into the atmosphere,
There's a chance a few will stay
Until later in the day,
Something else that you should know—
Make one wish before they go.

Daisy danced around the room. "I'm finally going to get a puppy!"

Eva leaned over the cookbook and read the magic cupcake charm again. "Sorry to burst your bubble, but it doesn't sound like they'll stick around for very long."

"But you're forgetting something." Daisy laughed. "I get to make a wish."

Molly's mouth split into a grin. "And you're going to wish that one will stay forever."

"Of course," said Daisy.

"Well, I guess that's one way to get what you want," said Eva. "But I still think you should show your mom that you've become more responsible, and then she'll get you a *real* puppy."

"But this sounds much easier," said Daisy.

"Woof, woof!" The Magic Cookbook barked impatiently.

"I agree," said Daisy. "Let's hurry up and make the pupcakes."

The girls worked together in the kitchen, preparing the cake batter and popping the chocolate chip banana cupcakes into the oven.

After the cupcakes were baked and cooled, frosting, candies, and craft supplies appeared on the big kitchen table.

Daisy spooned white frosting on a cupcake, added chocolate chip eyes, a brown M&M nose, and yogurt-covered almonds for the ears. She heaped shredded coconut on top so it looked very shaggy, and added a little Red Hot candy tongue. Then she made a dog tag out of yellow construction paper.

"He looks like a sheepdog puppy," Molly smiled.

"What's his name?" asked Eva.

"Ruffles," said Daisy, writing the name on the tag. "I've always thought that would be a good name for a shaggy sheepdog." She put a drop of frosting on the back of the tag and stuck it to the side of the pupcake. Then she added a blue ribbon collar.

Eva smoothed chocolate frosting onto a cupcake, added chocolate chip eyes, chocolate-covered almond ears, and a malt ball nose.

"He looks like a chocolate Labrador," said Molly.

"What's *his* name?" asked Daisy.

"Cocoa," said Eva, looking very pleased.

"This is my golden retriever named Pumpkin," said Molly, admiring the yellow cupcake with the almond ears, a chocolate kiss nose, and chocolate chip eyes.

The girls had tons of fun making their favorite breeds of dogs, and when there were just four cupcakes and a few decorations left, they made crazy, mismatched puppies.

"This one's a little scary," said Molly, as she held up a red cupcake with one green M&M eye and one yellow one. It had two candy corn fangs, a yogurt-covered almond snout, and two blue jellybean ears.

The girls put the entire litter of pupcakes on a cookie tray on the kitchen counter and then recited the magic cupcake charm. Then The Magic Cookbook vanished into the cupboard, and the door shut behind it. When Daisy opened it up again, the cookbook was nowhere to be seen.

"I wonder when the cupcakes will start to change," said Eva, eyeing the pupcakes.

"I have an idea," said Daisy. "Let's take our favorites into my room for the night. We can put them on our pillows."

"What if we accidentally roll on top of them and squash them?" asked Eva.

"We'll just have to be careful," said Daisy.

Eva rolled her eyes. "You? Careful?"

Daisy ignored her.

"What about the other twenty-one pupcakes? What should we do with those?" asked Molly.

"Let's leave them here on the tray, and we'll see them in the morning," said Daisy.

The girls grabbed Ruffles, Cocoa and Pumpkin, and went to Daisy's room.

"I can't wait to see what's going to happen," said Daisy as she snuggled into her sleeping bag on the floor between her friends. "Goodnight Ruffles," she said to the pupcake on her pillow.

"Goodnight Cocoa," said Eva.

"Goodnight Pumpkin," said Molly.

Hazel popped her head into the room. "Goodnight girls. I've got to leave early in the morning and get ready for another big day at the shop. Stop by and see me after breakfast sometime."

"All right," said Molly.

"Have fun with the pupcakes," whispered Hazel and then tiptoed away.

Daisy's eyes popped open. *Wait! How does she know about them?*

✳   ✳   ✳

As Daisy was just waking up the next morning, she felt something sticky and wet on her cheek. *Slurp!*

"What's that?" Eyes still closed, she reached up to wipe her face, and felt something furry next to her head. She opened her eyes just as a giant, red tongue came down from above and licked her on the lips. It sort of tasted like salty Red Hot candies.

Slurp!

"Ruffles," she cried. "You're alive!"

Molly and Eva bolted up in their sleeping bags.

"Did it happen, did it happen?" asked Eva. "Aw," she said as she reached out and stroked the sleeping chocolate Labrador puppy on her pillow. "He's so cute."

Molly put on her glasses. "Not as cute as Pumpkin." She rubbed noses with the sweet, yellow puppy.

"Let's go find the others," said Daisy. The girls threw on their clothes and dashed down the hall to the kitchen.

The tray of pupcakes was empty. "Where are they?" asked Molly.

"Maybe they've already disappeared," said Eva. "Or maybe," she bit her lip, "Ruffles ate them."

"Hey," said Daisy. "Why are you blaming Ruffles?"

"Well, just look at him," said Eva. "He's covered with crumbs."

Daisy squatted down on the floor and examined Ruffles. Eva was right. Ruffles had big crumbs on his snout. She hadn't noticed that before.

"I can't believe Ruffles would eat the others," said Daisy.

Ruffles licked his lips with his long, slurpy tongue and burped.

"He looks pretty guilty to me," said Eva.

"There's only one way to find out for sure," said Daisy, picking a crumb off of Ruffles's nose and putting it on her tongue.

"Ew, that's disgusting," said Eva.

"What does it taste like?" asked Molly.

"Salt," said Daisy. She scanned the kitchen and then laughed. "Look over there." A large box of saltine crackers was shredded to bits under the kitchen table.

Daisy patted Ruffles's shaggy head and then stopped. "Listen," she said.

Woof, woof, woof! Something was happening in the next room.

The girls threw open the kitchen door and ran into the living room, their three puppies close at their heels.

"Oh no," Daisy, Eva and Molly all said at once.

Puppies were running everywhere, jumping on tables, hanging on the chandelier, knocking over potted plants, and then scampering through the potting soil and tracking it all over the Persian carpet.

"My mom is going to kill me," said Daisy.

"She might kill us, too," said Molly. She ran over to the grand piano where two chubby black and white Dalmatians were pounding on the black and white keys and playing a duet that sounded like the old classic, *You Ain't Nothing But a Hound Dog.*

"Come on you little rascals," said Molly. Just as she reached out to grab them, they vanished, leaving a few chocolate chips behind on the piano keys.

"I'll get these guys before they track more dirt across the carpet," yelled Eva, cornering four pink poodles with very muddy paws. They looked like balls of cotton candy that had been dipped in milk chocolate. She took a step closer, and the poodles disappeared.

Five springer spaniels were sliding across the large dining room table. Daisy waited for them to skid into her open arms when, *Poof,* they were gone, leaving streaks of vanilla and chocolate frosting on the table.

"There aren't many pupcakes left," said Molly, after the six Saint Bernards that had been swinging from the chandelier fell to the floor and dissolved. Only their red licorice collars remained.

"Let's see," said Eva. "That was two Dalmatians, four poodles, five spaniels, and six Saint Bernards. That makes seventeen pupcakes."

Ruffles, Pumpkin and Cocoa are still with us," said Daisy, "so that makes twenty. Didn't we make four more?"

"I think so," said Molly, just before Ruffles, Cocoa and Pumpkin, jumped onto Mrs. Humphrey's beautiful, blue sofa. They grabbed the new silk pillow and began playing tug-of-war.

"Stop, stop," cried Daisy. "You've got to stop before you…"

Rrrrrriiiippp!

A cloud of feathers exploded. Pumpkin and Cocoa stared at the girls for a moment and then, *poof, poof,* they disappeared.

"That's sad," said Molly, and Eva nodded.

Ruffles sat on the couch with the remnants of the pillow in his mouth.

Daisy picked him up, and he nestled into her neck. A few flakes of coconut-scented fur stuck to Daisy's collar. "You really are a naughty little puppy," she said. "But, I'm awfully glad that you're still here. I want Hazel to meet you." Daisy headed for the front door.

"Shouldn't we clean up first?" Eva looked around the room. "It looks like a tornado hit."

"More like twenty tornadoes," said Daisy, forgetting that they still hadn't found the four missing puppies. Daisy scratched her head. "I guess you're right, Eva. Maybe we *should* clean up before going over to Hazel's."

After a quick breakfast, the girls got out brooms, dust cloths, sponges, cleansers, trash bags, and the heavy-duty vacuum cleaner. Then they cleaned the living room, while Ruffles took a nap in a patch of sunlight by the window.

"The room looks pretty good," said Eva an hour later. "Well, everything except the silk pillow."

Daisy nodded. "We've done what we can do, so let's go over to Hazel's now. There's still plenty of time before my mom and Arlo get home."

Ruffles ran out the door after Daisy and her friends. None of them noticed the four mismatched puppies that were lurking behind Mrs. Humphrey's large bookcase.

*   *   *

"He's just the cutest little puppy," said Hazel, as she scratched Ruffles behind the ears. "And he smells so delicious."

Ruffles squealed with delight and licked Hazel's hand. Then he ran over to the front door to greet customers.

"Don't forget to make a wish before he goes," said Hazel.

"I'm still working on it," said Daisy. "I want to come up with the perfect one."

"You could wish that he was already trained." Hazel nodded towards Ruffles who was jumping up on two little girls.

"I see what you mean," said Daisy, "but I think it'll be more fun if we train him ourselves." She strode towards Ruffles, swooped him up in her arms and carried him out to the front lawn next to the golf course.

For the next two hours, the girls trained Ruffles to come, stay, fetch golf balls, and sit. They even trained him to ignore Velvet when the cat ran around the golf course.

When Daisy rewarded Ruffles with tiny salmon from the Alaskan Wilderness, the little bear, who had grown quite pudgy, tried to run them off. "Be nice," said Daisy. "There's plenty for everyone."

And it was true. It seemed to Daisy that as soon as she fished one salmon out of the river, another one would appear in its place. "What a magical river. I wonder what else it can do."

Eva looked at her watch. "I've got to go home now."

"Me too," said Molly.

Daisy said goodbye to her friends, and then carried Ruffles back to The Honeysuckle Inn. "Mom and Arlo should be here any minute. Let's make sure that everything's still okay," said Daisy as she walked into the living room.

"Oh no!" she cried. "Who did this?" Coffee tables were turned upside down, the glass chandelier had fallen from the ceiling and shattered on the floor, muddy paw prints were all over the walls, and four crazed puppies were on top of the blue sofa and shredding it to bits.

"You bad, bad dogs!" cried Daisy.

Ruffles ran towards them and barked. The devilish dogs snarled, glared at Ruffles and Daisy with their eerie eyes, and then one by one they evaporated.

"And never come back," Daisy yelled after them. Ruffles barked again, as if making a point.

Then Daisy looked around the wrecked room. Her heart sank. "I'll never be able to clean this up on my own in time. My mom is going to freak out, and she'll never let me get a puppy, ever!"

Daisy scratched Ruffles behind the ears. "I guess I won't be able to wish for what I really want. Someday, I will get a puppy, and hopefully, he'll be as wonderful as you."

Ruffles sighed.

"I wish that this room would clean itself up, immediately," Daisy exclaimed.

A flash of green light streaked through the room, and a moment later, everything was spotless. The chandelier was hanging neatly from the ceiling, the blue sofa and silk pillow looked as good as new, and Ruffles was gone.

A few minutes later, Daisy's mom opened the front door and walked into the living room with Arlo. Mrs. Humphrey hugged her daughter. "We missed you, sweetie. I hope you had a good time here. What did you do?"

"Oh, nothing much," said Daisy. "Just a bit of cleaning."

"That was so sweet of you," said her mother. "It looks beautiful."

Something on the floor caught Daisy's eye. She leaned over and picked up the little, yellow nametag. *Ruffles.* A moment later, it disappeared.

Daisy sighed. *Wouldn't it be wonderful if I could see him again someday?*

Pupcakes

Magic Cupcake Charm
Little pupcakes everywhere,
Treats like these are very rare,
In the morning you'll have found
They've turned into special hounds,
One by one they'll disappear
Straight into the atmosphere,
There's a chance a few will stay
Until later in the day,
Something else that you should know—
Make one wish before they go.

Ingredients for 24 Cupcakes

1 (18.25 ounce) package	yellow cake mix
3	eggs
1 cup	mashed ripe bananas
1 cup	sour cream
1/4 cup	oil
1 (24 ounce) bag	miniature chocolate chips
24	cupcake papers

Topping

1 (16 ounce) tub	cream cheese frosting
1 (16 ounce) tub	chocolate frosting
	food coloring (any colors you want)
	an assortment of decorator's gels, shredded coconut, cake sprinkles, and candies like chocolate kisses, malt balls, chocolate and yogurt-covered peanuts, Red Hot candies, Candy Corns, fruit leather, etc. Construction paper is good for dog tags, and ribbons make great collars. Have fun!

Preparation

1. Preheat oven to 350 degrees.

2. Combine cake mix, eggs, mashed bananas, sour cream, and oil in a large bowl. Beat at medium speed for 4 minutes. Stir in one-half bag of chocolate chips.

3. Line the muffin tins with cupcake papers and fill three-quarters full with batter. Put the cupcakes in the oven. Bake 17 to 20 minutes. Set aside to cool.

4. Set up a pupcake decorating area large enough to spread out your frostings, candies, cake sprinkles, etc. Divide the cream cheese frosting into bowls and dye different colors with food coloring. Frost and decorate your pupcakes.

When you've finished making these treats, recite the charm so that they're complete.

July

On the Fourth of July, Daisy and her friends were at The Honeysuckle Inn drinking lemonade and waiting for The Magic Cookbook. Through the back kitchen window, the girls could see Arlo and Dexter jumping on the trampoline, bouncing each other higher and higher.

Eva turned to her friends. "The cookbook had better show up soon. Otherwise we won't have time to make cupcakes for your mom's picnic tonight."

"It'll come," said Daisy. "It just has to."

Daisy's mom strolled into the kitchen. "I'm sorry to tell you this girls, but the town's fireworks have been cancelled this year."

"What?" Daisy and her friends cried.

"Unfortunately, the fireworks were in a storage room under a leaky pipe, and they were ruined." Mrs. Humphrey continued, "Also, Hazel just called. She has a cold and won't be able to come tonight."

Daisy's mom gave each of the girls a hug. "Cheer up, we'll still have fun. I'll go check on Hazel to make sure she's okay. Then I'll be on the back patio setting up for the picnic." The back door swung shut behind her.

"Oh well, at least we still have The Magic Cookbook," said Daisy.

"That is, if it ever shows up," said Eva. "We've been waiting for a long time."

"Maybe it's inside of a cupboard like last time," said Molly, and the girls opened up all of the cupboard doors and poked their heads inside.

"Nope," said Daisy, and then scratched her head. "I wonder where it could be."

POP, POP, POP. Suddenly, red, white and blue sparks exploded from the trashcan in the corner. A moment later, The Magic Cookbook shot out of it like a cannonball, sailed across the room and landed on the counter.

The girls clapped, and the book flipped open to a recipe for Campfire Cupcakes.

Campfire Cupcakes–
They're rockets in disguise,
It'll be a blast–
They're full of surprise,
When the sun goes down
And the day is done,
That's when these cupcakes
Really have some fun!

Daisy, Molly and Eva sprang into action. After they mixed up the cupcake batter, they poured it into the cup-sized graham cracker piecrusts that had appeared on the counter. Then they plopped a chocolate kiss in the center of each one. Once baked and cooled, the girls frosted the cupcakes with chocolate frosting. They stuck miniature marshmallows on pretzel sticks, then arranged them on top of the cupcakes to look like little campfires. They placed a birthday candle in the center of each one.

After Daisy and her friends recited the magic cupcake charm, the cookbook shot across the room and disappeared, leaving a trail of exploding sparks behind.

Daisy's mom dashed into the room. "What in the world is going on in here? It sounds like fireworks are going off."

"Just making cupcakes for tonight," said Daisy.

"Well, I can't wait to see them," said Mrs. Humphrey with a confused look on her face. "They must be very exciting."

* * *

That night at the party, Daisy, Eva, and Molly sat at the kids' table with Arlo and Dexter.

"Watch my new magic trick," said Arlo. "I'm going to make this food disappear." He gobbled up a biscuit and a piece of fried chicken, then smiled.

Dexter burst out laughing. "That's your best trick so far."

"Cute," said Eva, rolling her eyes.

Molly and Eva's parents were sitting together at one end of the adults' table, close enough for the girls to hear them.

"I sure wish we could watch fireworks this evening," said Eva's father, Mr. Perez. "This will be our first year without them."

Mr. McGregor shook his head. "It's been an unusual year in Willow Brook." Then he paused. "Remember the big blizzard back in January?"

Mrs. Perez nodded. "It was incredible."

"And no one could ever really explain what happened," said Mrs. McGregor.

Daisy, Molly and Eva exchanged glances.

"Maybe we should serve the cupcakes so they'll stop talking about this," whispered Daisy. Her friends nodded.

Daisy strode to the refreshment table and with her mother's help, lit the birthday candles on half of the campfire cupcakes. Then she picked up a pretzel stick from the top of a cupcake and checked to make sure the mini-marshmallow was securely fastened at one end.

Daisy turned to the guests. "Okay everybody, this is how you do this." Daisy held the marshmallow over the candle flame until it was perfectly roasted. She laughed when red, white and blue sparks sizzled over the cupcake like a sparkler. The kids cheered and the adults clapped.

"Pretty clever," said Mrs. Humphrey, passing the platter of cupcakes around to the delighted guests. She set the remaining cupcakes on the kids' table and smiled at Daisy. "Honey, you keep an eye on these until we're ready to have more."

Mrs. Humphrey returned to her seat.

"The cupcakes taste just like S'mores," said Molly. "Chocolate, marshmallow and graham crackers are a great combo."

"But I really expected more than just good taste and sparks," said Daisy.

"I know what you mean," agreed Eva. "The magic cupcake charm made it sound much more exciting."

"Oh well," said Daisy. "I guess not every cupcake recipe is going to blow our socks off." *Perhaps another round will help,* she thought as she carefully lit the candles on the remaining cupcakes. Before she could pass the plate around though, Daisy stumbled and fell, and the Campfire Cupcakes flew through the air and came crashing down on the nearby trampoline.

"Oh, Daisy," said Molly. "What a shame."

"Look!" Daisy pointed at the trampoline a moment later. The cupcakes were jumping.

"Wow," said Eva. "Their candles are still lit."

"And they're bouncing each other up and down," said Arlo.

"Just like we did earlier," said Dexter. "Awesome."

With each bounce the cupcakes flew higher and higher, until a few minutes later, they rocketed upward and hovered in the air. Silver lightning bolts burst out of the cupcakes, streaked across the sky, and rumbled.

The girls gasped, and the adults finally looked up from their conversation. "This is amazing," said one of the guests. "Your town puts on quite a fireworks display."

"Mommy, you told me we weren't having them this year," said Arlo.

Purple balls of fire shot into the sky, swirling faster and faster. Smaller circles formed nearby—yellow circles, blue and red circles, twirling and twirling. Then there was a loud BOOM, and dozens of pink and orange twinkling stars exploded into the middle of the swirling lights.

A gust of wind came up out of nowhere, and huge sparks rained from the sky.

"Oh, it's so beauti...," Molly stopped mid-sentence as the sparks began to shower directly onto Blake's Rare Books. For a moment there was complete silence, then everyone ran next door where the front porch was already in flames. Hazel and Velvet were nowhere to be seen.

"Where's Hazel's hose?" yelled Molly.

"It's over there, but it's too close to the fire." Eva pointed at the hose next to the burning porch.

"I'm going to call the fire department," shouted Mrs. Humphrey, but Daisy knew that if they waited much longer it would be too late. What on Earth could they do? Who could possibly help them now? Suddenly, Daisy remembered the last two lines of the Goofy Golf Cupcake magic charm. *Over time and more than once, this course could save the day, but only if you're listening to what I have to say.*

Daisy concentrated like she had never concentrated before. She knew exactly what to do. She faced the golf course and shouted, "Help! Help! Help!"

Instantly the course sprang into action. The Colorado River rushed full force out of the Grand Canyon and towards the burning porch. Las Vegas's towering fountains blasted the fire, and the cloud over the Amazon Rainforest grew and poured buckets and buckets of rain. Out of the corner of her eye, Daisy saw the little bear from the Alaskan Wilderness ride a wave over to Niagara Falls and turn the knob on full force. Mammoth amounts of mist drenched the fire until the flames were completely out.

The goofy golf course shut itself off, just as the side door of the bookstore opened. Hazel emerged with Velvet in her arms. When she saw the charred porch and all of the drenched people, she said, "Oh my."

"Thank goodness you're okay!" The girls rushed to her side.

"Gracious me. I wasn't feeling well and went to bed early. Then I heard someone yelling for help and came outside to see what all of the commotion was about. What happened?"

When Eva explained how Daisy and the golf course had come to the rescue, Hazel said, "Daisy, your concentration and quick thinking saved Velvet and me, and the bookstore too. We are so grateful."

Hazel kissed Daisy on the cheek, and Velvet rubbed up against her legs.

Everyone went back to The Honeysuckle Inn for homemade peach ice cream and to watch Arlo and Dexter's magic show.

Campfire Cupcakes

Magic Cupcake Charm
Campfire Cupcakes-
They're rockets in disguise,
It'll be a blast-
They're full of surprise,
When the sun goes down
And the day is done,
That's when these cupcakes
Really have some fun!

Ingredients for 24 Cupcakes

1 (18.25 ounce) package	yellow cake mix
4	eggs
1/3 cup	oil
1 cup	water
24	chocolate candy kisses
24	miniature graham cracker piecrusts (*or* 1 box of graham crackers and 24 cupcake papers)

Topping

1 (16 ounce) tub	chocolate frosting
1 (10 ounce) bag	miniature marshmallows
1 bag	stick pretzels (you need about 100 pretzels)
24	birthday candles

Preparation

1. Preheat oven to 350°F.

2. Combine the cake mix, eggs, oil and water in a large bowl. Beat at medium speed for 4 minutes. Spoon the batter into the miniature graham cracker piecrusts*. Fill two-thirds full and put a

chocolate kiss in the middle of each one. Put them on a cookie sheet and bake for 15 minutes or until done. Set aside to cool.

3. Frost the cupcakes with chocolate frosting. Stick marshmallows on the ends of the pretzels and build a miniature campfire on each cupcake. Before serving, put a birthday candle in the middle of each cupcake and light them with the help of an adult. Try roasting the mini-marshmallows over the flame.

When you've finished making these treats, recite the charm so that they're complete.

Baker's Note

*If you can't find miniature graham cracker piecrusts, use a rolling pin to mash graham crackers. Sprinkle these in the bottom of the cupcake papers before filling them with batter.

August

O n the morning of Daisy's eleventh birthday, the girls sat in the kitchen of The Honeysuckle Inn. "This has been the best summer ever. Too bad it's almost over," said Daisy.

"You know you've changed a lot," said Eva. "You're much more responsible now."

"Really?" Daisy was delighted. "I've been working on it."

"I can tell," said Molly. "You've been a huge help at the golf course."

"Well, I love fixing things, so it's been great," said Daisy.

"I know what else has been great," said Molly. "We haven't seen Tiffany for two whole months."

Eva nodded and then asked, "So Daisy, what do you want to do today for your birthday?"

Daisy walked over to the kitchen sink. "Hmm," she said. "It's got to be something really special." Daisy turned on the faucet to wash her empty orange juice glass, but no water came out of the spout. She turned the faucet on a bit more, but still nothing happened.

"Maybe something's stuck inside," said Daisy just before she heard a loud sputtering sound.

"I think pressure is building up," said Eva.

"It's getting louder. Something's about to come spewing out," said Molly.

A moment later The Magic Cookbook squeezed out of the spout, followed by a torrent of water.

Daisy quickly turned off the faucet and looked at the cookbook in the sink. It was long and skinny and very, very wet. While Daisy was toweling it off, the cookbook returned to its normal size and jumped over to the counter.

"I'm so glad that it showed up for my last turn," said Daisy, "and what a cool entrance."

Then the book flipped open to a page that was covered with sand. Daisy brushed it off, and a magic cupcake charm for Sand Castle Cupcakes appeared.

Ever longed for the beach but it's too far away?
Here's your chance to go there now—it's your lucky day.
Make these cupcakes, take a bite—soon you will find out,
What magical sand castles really are about.

"Awesome," said Daisy. "Let's get started."

"We have something we want to give you first," said Eva, and she and Molly handed Daisy a present.

Daisy unwrapped it and saw a bright orange and yellow striped apron. "Is this a hint?" She giggled and slipped it on over her shorts and t-shirt.

"This is for you, too," said Molly as she handed her friend a card that she'd painted with eleven puppies on the front.

Daisy hugged her friends, and then they got to work making the lemon-flavored cupcake batter, pouring it into flat-bottomed ice cream cones that were sitting on a pan, and putting them in the oven to bake.

After the cupcakes were cooled and frosted, Daisy smashed up the Vanilla Wafer cookies that had appeared on the counter. Eva and Molly frosted pointed ice cream cones and rolled them in the cookie crumbs. Then they turned them upside down and placed them on top of the cupcakes.

"They really do look like sand castles," said Eva, slipping a Lifesaver candy on each cone tip. After reciting the magic cupcake charm with her friends, The Magic Cookbook rushed back to the kitchen sink and disappeared down the drain.

"What an exit," said Daisy. "I wish it had stuck around longer so I could say goodbye."

"Don't worry," said Eva. "You'll see it next month when it's my turn to have it."

Daisy nodded and then reached for the phone. "Well, since it sounds like we're going to the beach, I'm calling Hazel to see if she wants to join us."

"I'll close the store and the golf course for the afternoon," said Hazel, a minute later. "I could use a relaxing break. Come over when you're ready."

The girls filled a picnic basket with the cupcakes, some sandwiches and sodas, and then rushed next door to Blake's Rare Books.

Hazel had a big umbrella tucked under her arm and a beach bag slung over her shoulder. "Daisy, please hand me one of the Sand Castle Cupcakes."

"How do you know about them?" asked Daisy as she plucked a cupcake out of the picnic basket.

"Just a hunch." A sly smile crossed Hazel's lips as she broke four chunks off of the cupcake and handed one to each of the girls. "Take a bite and away we'll go."

Eva looked concerned. "Are you sure?"

Hazel nodded. "Come along, dear. We don't have all day." Hazel popped her treat into her mouth. The girls all did the same, and before any of them could say, *Sand Castle Cupcakes*, they were standing on warm, wet sand, looking out at the clear, blue ocean. Seagulls were gliding in the breeze, waves crashed on the shore, and rays of sunlight pierced through the light fog that hung in the air. They were the only people in a beautiful secluded cove.

"We're at the beach," Daisy shouted. "I love the beach!"

"Me too," said Hazel. "And this is one of my favorites. It's called, Cupcake Cove." She put up her umbrella and spread a blanket out across the warm sand. Then Hazel handed all but five of the cupcakes to the girls. "I'm saving four of these for our dessert."

"What's the other one for?" asked Daisy.

"To transport us home," said Hazel.

"You've obviously done this before," said Eva. "I feel better now that I know we can leave."

"What should we do with the other cupcakes?" Molly wanted to know.

"Let's make a sand castle with them," said Daisy.

The girls ran to the water's edge and started building. They pressed the cupcakes into the castle walls and added them to the corners.

"The cupcakes make perfect towers," said Eva.

"That was a great idea, Daisy," said Molly.

Hazel walked over and admired the sand castle. Seagull feathers lined a path that led to the driftwood drawbridge that crossed over the moat. Pink, white and blue seashells decorated the walls and were strewn about the courtyard.

Daisy removed the Lifesaver candies from four of the cupcakes and set them next to the moat. "Let's pretend that they're inner tubes," she said.

After they finished eating their picnic lunch, Hazel led the girls down the beach to a lighthouse. It was still a bit foggy, but they could see a huge house up on a bluff.

"Whoever lives up there is really lucky," said Molly.

Twenty minutes later, they turned around and walked back to Cupcake Cove. They could see Hazel's orange umbrella in the distance, and there was something else. Something that hadn't been there before.

"It's hard to see through the fog, but it looks like some kind of house," said Eva.

"Or maybe a castle," cried Daisy. "Let's go see."

The girls took off in a sprint, and Hazel strolled behind, smiling.

"It's our sand castle!" said Molly and Eva at the same time.

"Whoa," yelled Daisy. "It's huge!"

Hazel arrived a minute later. "Oh my, this has to be one of the biggest sand castles I've ever seen. Those must be very magical Sand Castle Cupcakes indeed."

The castle looked exactly like the one the girls had made earlier, but it was at least fifteen feet tall. The moat, the driftwood drawbridge, the shells and feathers—they were all enormous. The cupcake towers soared above everything and sparkled in the sun. It really was an impressive sight.

"Oh look," said Molly. "The Lifesavers next to the moat are like big inner tubes now!"

"Awesome!" Daisy slid one into the water and climbed aboard. Eva and Molly did the same.

"Come on in, Hazel," the girls urged.

Hazel sat on top of a red Lifesaver, pushed off from the sandy shore and glided into the water. "I haven't done anything like this in years." Hazel giggled like a school-girl. Then the four of them drifted in the gentle current around the castle.

"This is amazing." Daisy splashed.

After floating around the castle twice, Eva eyed her dissolving Lifesaver. "I think we'd better get out soon. My inner tube is getting smaller and stickier by the minute."

Reluctantly, everybody climbed out of the moat and dried off.

"Let's explore the inside of the castle," said Hazel. "But first, let's pack up our things and carry them with us. Just in case."

"Just in case of what?" asked Daisy.

"Just humor me, sweetheart."

They walked across the driftwood drawbridge and through the front entrance of the remarkable building. A long hallway ran along the outside edge of the castle, and the courtyard in the center was filled with the dazzling shells that were now as large as boulders.

Hazel held her finger up to her lips. "Shhhh."

They could hear a girl's voice from outside the castle walls. "Look at this. It reminds me of the cake I made for Valentine's Day."

"You mean the one that Jacques made?" another girl asked.

"Oh, be quiet Jessica, and take a picture of me in front of the castle. I'm going to tell everyone in our class that I made it. Maybe that will show Daisy, Eva and Molly. They think they're so great."

The voices faded for a moment.

Daisy stared at her friends. Had they really ended up on the beach where the Burnsleys had a summer home?

"I've heard enough," whispered Hazel. She unpacked the last Sand Castle Cupcake and handed everyone a section. Hazel, Molly, and Eva quickly ate theirs and disappeared.

Daisy tossed her piece up to her mouth and almost caught it. It plummeted to the ground at exactly the same moment that the remaining fog lifted, and Tiffany walked into the courtyard and screamed.

"What are you doing here?" She marched over to Daisy.

Daisy smiled. "Oh, hi Tiffany. Small world, isn't it?" She knelt down in search of her cupcake.

"What are you doing here?" demanded Tiffany again.

"I'm just looking for this." Daisy picked up her magic morsel, dusted the sand off and popped the cupcake successfully into her mouth. She waved goodbye to Tiffany and disappeared.

When she landed back at Blake's Rare Books, Daisy was laughing so hard that her friends had to wait a full five minutes before she could tell them what had happened. "The look on Tiffany's face was hilarious," she said.

"I wish I'd seen it," said Eva.

"Not me," said Molly. "I'll see Tiffany when school starts in September."

"Which is very, very soon," said Daisy. Then she gazed around the bookstore and called out, "Thank you Magic Cookbook, wherever you are."

Velvet dashed out from behind a bookshelf and circled through Daisy's legs. Daisy leaned over and scratched his head. "Silly cat. *You're* not The Magic Cookbook."

Velvet gazed up at Daisy and purred.

As the girls climbed down the new wooden steps of Hazel's recently repaired porch, there was a bright flash of light, and the miniature golf course disappeared.

Daisy turned to her friends. "Well, I guess that means that summer really is over."

Daisy said goodbye to her friends, and then walked back to The Honeysuckle Inn.

*   *   *

After a delicious birthday dinner with her family, Daisy's mom handed her a gift. "Here, sweetheart."

Daisy tore off the wrapping paper. There was the book, *How to Raise A Puppy.*

"And there's one more thing." Arlo beamed. "We've been keeping it a secret."

"What is it?" asked Daisy hopefully.

Mrs. Humphrey handed Daisy a much larger box from under the table.

Daisy yanked off the lid. A sheepdog puppy popped out, jumped into Daisy's lap and licked her face over and over again.

"Oh, he's perfect. Thank you so much," Daisy cried. "Where did you find him, Mom?"

"When I saw how much more responsible you were getting, I decided to find you a puppy for your birthday. I went to a few pet shops, but didn't have any luck. Then yesterday, Hazel showed me an ad in *The Willow Brook Times* for sheepdog puppies. When Arlo and I went to look at them, we fell in love with this little guy and brought him home."

"He slept in Mommy's room last night," said Arlo.

"He really is a wonderful puppy," said Mrs. Humphrey. "You certainly deserve him."

Daisy scratched the puppy behind the ears and then nuzzled her face into his fur.

"Here's one more gift," said Mrs. Humphrey. "It's from Hazel."

Daisy opened the little box and smiled. Inside was a blue collar with a yellow tag attached. It said, *Ruffles.*

Sand Castle Cupcakes

Magic Cupcake Charm
Ever longed for the beach but it's too far away?
Here's your chance to go there now—it's your lucky day.
Make these cupcakes, take a bite—soon you will find out,
What magical sand castles really are about!

Ingredients for 24 Cupcakes

1 (18.25 ounce) package	lemon cake mix
1 & 1/4 cup	buttermilk
1/3 cup	oil
3	eggs
24	old-fashioned ice cream cones (with flat bottoms)

Topping

2 (16 ounce) tubs	white frosting
	yellow food coloring
24	sugar cones (ice cream cones with pointed tips)
1 box	Vanilla Wafer cookies
24	Lifesavers
1	large Ziploc bag

Preparation

1. Preheat oven to 350 degrees.
2. In a large bowl, combine cake mix, buttermilk, oil and eggs. Beat at medium speed for 4 minutes.
3. Put a flat-bottomed ice cream cone in each of the muffin tin cups. Fill each cone about two-thirds full with batter or approximately one inch from

the top. Put the cupcakes in the oven. Bake 15 to 18 minutes. Set aside to cool.

4. Color the frosting yellow and frost cupcakes. Put the Vanilla Wafer cookies in a re-sealable plastic bag and use a rolling pin or the side of a can to crush them. Pour the crumbs onto a cookie sheet.

5. Frost the pointed sugar cones with a thin layer of frosting and roll them in cookie crumbs. Arrange the cupcakes on the baking sheet with the remaining cookie crumbs on it. Put a Lifesaver on the tip of each sugar cone. Cupcakes will look like sand castles at the beach.

When you've finished making these treats, recite the charm so that they're complete.

PART 3

Eva

All your ducks are in a row,
You're so smart from head to toe,
Always heading towards your goal,
Just relax and lose control.

september

It was the first day of school, and the fifth graders were sitting in their desks waiting for Mr. Vine to arrive.

"I can't believe that he's late," said Eva. "Maybe he's watching us on a hidden camera to see if we're behaving." She sat up straighter.

"What a creepy thought." Molly stopped drawing on her notebook, then adjusted her glasses and looked around.

"Maybe he won't show up at all," said Daisy. "Wouldn't that be wonderful?"

"But if he doesn't show up there might not be a holiday fair in December. I've been looking forward to being in charge of it for ages," said Eva.

"We know," said Daisy. "You mention it practically every day."

"I'm just really clear about what I want," Eva huffed.

A minute later, Mrs. Parker, the principal, walked in. "I have an announcement to make. We recently got word that Mr. Vine won't be teaching this year."

The fifth graders all began asking questions.

"One at a time please," said Mrs. Parker.

"Why did he quit?" asked Josh Wiley.

"He and Miss Plum got married over the summer and have moved away."

The children giggled.

"Seriously?" asked Jake Farmer.

"Yes, seriously," Mrs. Parker replied, and then looked at Eva who was flailing her arm in the air. "Yes, Miss Perez?"

"Is there still going to be a holiday fair, and if so, will one of us be chosen to organize it?"

"Most definitely," said Mrs. Parker. "The fair is a school tradition."

Eva breathed a sigh of relief.

"Are we going to have a teacher this year?" asked Daisy.

"You certainly are, and here he is."

Eva held her breath. The door to the classroom swung open, and Mr. Clark strode in. The children cheered and clapped. Mrs. Parker smiled and then ducked out of the room.

"Hello," said Mr. Clark. "I'm glad to see you all again, too. I guess I'm not meant to retire for another year."

When the cheering died down, Mr. Clark continued. "I'd like to start the year in a fun way. Our class will have a bake sale right after lunch on Monday. The money will go towards the holiday fair."

Eva smiled. *Everything is going my way, and it's my turn with The Magic Cookbook. I know it will help me get what I want.*

Out of the corner of her eye, Eva saw something big and gray. She turned and looked out the window next to her desk. Velvet was sitting on the outside ledge watching her. Eva smiled at him but then started feeling nervous. *Why is he staring at me like that?*

* * *

That Sunday afternoon, Eva scoured her kitchen, leaving the counters, cabinets and appliances sparkling. She even washed the window that faced the driveway, and the larger one that faced the old barn in her family's big backyard.

Eva smiled. *I'm so excited for The Magic Cookbook to show up. Mom and Dad are next door in their flower shop, so my friends and I will have the kitchen to ourselves. Everything is going to be perfect for my first turn.*

A few minutes later, Molly and Daisy arrived, with Ruffles following behind them.

"I didn't know that he would be here, too," said Eva. "I hope he can stay out of our way while we bake cupcakes."

Daisy glanced down at her puppy. "Go lie down, Ruffles."

Immediately Ruffles walked over to the corner and settled down under the kitchen table.

Eva was impressed. "You've done an amazing job training him."

"Of course," said Daisy, smiling.

"This is for you, Eva," said Molly, as she handed her friend a white dishtowel that was covered with beautiful hand-painted flowers. "I made this for you."

"That's so sweet of you," said Eva.

"I've been making them for my mom's catering business, and I thought you could use one when you bake cupcakes," said Molly.

Eva was in a wonderful mood. She hummed as she got out muffin tins, bowls, measuring cups and spoons. She put on her apron and then looked around the kitchen and called, "Come out, come out, wherever you are."

Ruffles perked up his ears and peered at Eva.

"Sorry Ruffles," she said. "I wasn't talking to you."

"Are you calling The Magic Cookbook?" asked Daisy.

"Yes," said Eva as she peeked inside cupboards and drawers, and even up the kitchen sink spout. "Where is it?"

"If it doesn't show up soon, you could go over to Hazel's and get a book from her give-away bin," Daisy suggested. "That's how The Magic Cookbook came to me the first time."

Eva bit her lip. "Hmm. I didn't think of that."

"You don't need to go over there yet," said Molly. "It'll show up if you're patient."

"But I hate being patient. It feels like such a waste of time," said Eva, continuing to look around the kitchen. Then she pointed above the cabinets. "Look up there. It's stuck to the ceiling."

"Maybe it's been up there all day waiting for you," said Molly.

"What a horrible thought. I hate to keep anyone waiting." Eva rushed to the pantry, grabbed a broom, and gently knocked the book down with the handle. The book fell and landed on the counter, then flipped open. Eva read the poem that had materialized.

> The final four months of baking starts now,
> I have reappeared but no one knows how,
> This beautiful home is where we will meet,
> To make the best cupcakes you'll ever eat.
>
> Be sure to have fun when mixing batter,
> Top bakers know this really does matter,
> And just to be sure their treats have good taste,
> They all take their time, there's no need for haste.
>
> These magical treats are just what you need,
> To make you happy and help you succeed,
> Even in moments when you've lost your way,
> You'll have a friend who will make it okay.

Then the book turned to a new page. Strings of syrupy goo clung to it.

"Ew," said Eva.

She dampened a sponge and wiped it over the sticky page. The cookbook hissed and pulled away from her.

"I don't think it likes to get wet," said Molly.

"But I have to get this disgusting stuff off," said Eva as she approached the cookbook with the sponge again, and again, and again. But each time she got close, The Magic Cookbook backed away to another part of the counter.

Five minutes later, Eva groaned. "This is exhausting. At this rate we won't get started before my parents come in and start cooking dinner."

"Are they next door in their shop?" asked Daisy.

"They're *always* next door in their shop," Eva replied. "I keep telling them to hire help and to get a computer. They're working much harder than they need to because they aren't organized. It's driving me crazy."

"Well, their flower arrangements are beautiful," Molly reminded her. "And, they're so lucky that their business is attached to your house. They're close by—that must make it a bit easier."

Eva nodded, and turned back to the cookbook, glaring. "Just sit still for a minute. Please."

Ruffles rushed over to Eva and sat at her feet.

Eva patted his head. "Sorry Ruffles. I'm talking to the cookbook, not to you."

"I'll try one more time," said Eva. She reached towards the sticky page with the sponge. The brown goo rolled into a ball, and the cookbook coughed. The ball catapulted off the blank page, flew past Eva's head and landed with a SPLAT on the sage green wall.

"Oh no," said Eva. "We need to clean that up."

Ruffles dashed over.

"I didn't mean you," said Eva. She watched the puppy stand on his hind legs and lick the sweet sticky spot until it was gone. Eva patted him on the head. "Thanks Ruffles."

The puppy panted, and then went back to his place under the table and fell asleep.

"I wish The Magic Cookbook was as well-trained as Ruffles," said Eva. "This is not going the way I'd planned."

Eva felt a draft and turned to look at the window above the sink. She gasped when she saw that it was opening all by itself. "You guys, look!"

A stream of orange and red words were blowing in through the window and across the room. They drifted down to the open cookbook, forming a recipe for Sticky Caramel Apple Cupcakes.

Molly smiled. "That was incredibly cool."

Eva read the poem aloud.

> Here's a spin-off of an old tasty treat,
> That's tan and sticky and so very sweet.
> For those who are kind, with no lies to tell,
> Bite into a cupcake and all will go well.
> But if you are rude or have a cold heart,
> Your mouth will stick shut and won't come apart.
> If this does happen, you might have some luck,
> After five minutes it could come unstuck.
> You should examine what happened to you,
> With this sweet caramel that acted like glue,
> And then perhaps you might just realize—
> Telling the truth is its own perfect prize.

When the three girls finished baking the applesauce spice cupcakes, they dipped them in caramel sauce, and stuck a Popsicle stick into the center of each one. After they recited the magic cupcake charm, tiny balls of caramel shot through the air and splattered the tiled floor.

"You can help me now, Ruffles," said Eva, and the puppy ran around the room, licking up the sweet caramel until the floor was spotless.

Eva heard the front door open and footsteps walking down the hall. A moment later, her parents entered the kitchen.

"What adorable cupcakes, girls. They look like caramel apples," said Mrs. Perez. "Can we have a tiny taste?"

Eva wasn't so sure. "Sorry, but I think we need to save them all for the bake sale."

"Oh come on. Let's all share one," said Daisy.

"I think it'll be okay, Eva," said Molly, taking another look at the cupcakes.

"But what if our mouths get stuck shut?" Eva hadn't meant to blurt that out.

Her parents laughed.

"Sweetie," said her mom, "I don't think one bite will kill us."

"And if everyone promises to brush their teeth tonight, we'll be just fine." Mr. Perez winked at the girls.

"Well, okay," said Eva. She sliced up a cupcake and gave everyone a piece, including Ruffles. Eva watched them all take their first bites, then chew, swallow and open their mouths again.

"Delicious," said Mr. Perez.

"Delightful," said Mrs. Perez.

"Yummy," said Daisy.

"Woof," barked Ruffles.

"It's great," said Molly. "Go ahead Eva, eat yours."

Eva thought about the lines of the magic cupcake charm. *For those who are kind, with no lies to tell, Bite into a cupcake and all will go well.*

Eva thought for a moment. She knew that she was very kind

and never told lies. She took a little bite. Then, when she was one hundred percent sure that she could open her mouth again, she sighed with relief.

* * *

The next day at school, the fifth graders were in the corridor just outside the cafeteria setting up for the bake sale. They sat behind a long table filled with their treats, waiting for the other classes to get out of lunch. Lined up alongside the Sticky Caramel Apple Cupcakes were oatmeal cookies, brownies, pumpkin and pecan pies, blueberry muffins, and dark chocolate fudge. Tiffany sat in back of a beautiful miniature wedding cake with candy doves on top. "I'm asking $10 a slice."

"Tiffany, why don't you think about charging less so that students can afford to buy a piece," Mr. Clark suggested.

"I can't do that," she pouted. "It's a French recipe and worth a lot."

"I'm sure that Jacques made it for her, and she's taking all the credit again," whispered Eva.

"She's always taking credit for things she had nothing to do with," said Daisy. "Just like the sand castle last month."

"Someone needs to teach her a lesson," said Molly.

Mr. Clark strode to one end of the table. "The other classes will arrive any moment. I'll collect the money down here. Good luck fifth graders."

There was a thundering of footsteps, as children ran out of the cafeteria and made a beeline for the bake sale.

Eva watched as students ate the Sticky Caramel Apple Cupcakes. A few minutes later she smiled. "So far so good."

"Nobody's mouth is sticking shut," said Molly.

"Maybe the cupcakes aren't really magic," said Eva.

"Or maybe the children who are eating them aren't liars," said Daisy. "Like you-know-who."

Eva glanced over at Tiffany. She looked miserable. Her beautiful cake was completely untouched. Nobody had bought a single slice, and the bake sale appeared to be over.

It serves her right, thought Eva.

As if she could read Eva's thoughts, Tiffany looked up and glared.

Breaking eye contact, Eva turned her head away and looked at the one remaining Sticky Caramel Apple Cupcake on the platter in front of her.

"Let's share this last one," Eva said to Daisy and Molly.

But as she reached for the final cupcake, someone else's hand closed over it first.

Eva looked up from her chair. Tiffany was looming over her, and she was opening her mouth to bite into the cupcake.

"Hey, you need to pay for that before you eat it," said Eva.

Tiffany hesitated. "I did pay for it. You just weren't paying attention." Then Tiffany took a giant bite and began to chew.

For a moment, everything seemed okay. Eva thought that Tiffany was going to open her mouth and take another bite, but instead, Tiffany made a loud, shrill moaning sound.

Everyone froze. Tiffany made the noise again, only louder this time.

Mr. Clark rushed over. "What's wrong, Tiffany?"

Tiffany squealed.

Eva's heart was beating fast. It seemed that the harder Tiffany tried to open her mouth, the more trouble she was in. There was no doubt about it—Tiffany's mouth was glued shut with caramel.

All she could do was make the strange noise that grew louder and louder.

"What's happening to you, Tiffany?" asked Mr. Clark.

Caramel oozed from the corners of Tiffany's mouth, down her chin and onto her pink blouse.

"Maybe Mrs. Parker can help." Mr. Clark raced down the hall to the principal's office.

Eva looked at her friends. Molly and Daisy were both laughing so hard they fell off their chairs.

Eva wondered if she should help Tiffany. That's what someone who wanted to be chosen to organize the holiday fair would do. But instead, Eva lost control and laughed so hard that she fell off of her chair, too.

Tiffany flailed her arms around and knocked into her precious cake. After it plunged to the ground, the cake blew apart, and the candy doves hit the wall and shattered into tiny pieces.

"She really does love to smash things." Daisy giggled.

Eva had been following the second hand on the hall clock. After exactly five minutes, Tiffany's mouth sprang open. She wailed, "That was awful. What was in that cupcake anyway?"

"You mean the cupcake that you didn't pay for?" asked Eva.

Tiffany rubbed her jaw. "Yes, that awful cupcake. And believe me, I'm really sorry that I ever took it from you." Eva was surprised to see tears running down Tiffany's cheeks.

Mrs. Parker and Mr. Clark strode towards Tiffany. "Are you okay?"

"Of course I'm okay," said Tiffany. "But my mouth is sore."

"And our ears are sore from listening to your weird noises," Jake Farmer muttered.

Everyone stared as Tiffany marched past her demolished cake, down the hall and outside to the playground for recess. Eva noticed that for once, Jessica Jones didn't follow after her.

Eva turned to her friends, "I think this might be my favorite batch of magic cupcakes so far. They were messy, but they actually got Tiffany to apologize. Maybe she *has* learned a lesson."

Eva noticed a spot of sticky caramel on her wrist. She was about to wipe it off with a napkin but stopped. *I'll pretend I'm Ruffles.* Eva brought her wrist to her lips, and licked. *Yum.*

Sticky Caramel Apple Cupcakes

Magic Cupcake Charm
Here's a spin-off of an old tasty treat,
That's tan and sticky and so very sweet.
For those who are kind, with no lies to tell,
Bite into a cupcake and all will go well.
But if you are rude or have a cold heart,
Your mouth will stick shut and won't come apart.
If this does happen, you might have some luck,
After five minutes, it could come unstuck.
You should examine what happened to you,
With this sweet caramel that acted like glue,
And then perhaps you might just realize-
Telling the truth is its own perfect prize.

Ingredients for 24 Cupcakes

1 (18.25 ounce) package	spice cake mix (or yellow cake)
3	eggs
2 cups	applesauce
24	cupcake papers

Topping

40	caramel candies (or 1 jar caramel sauce)
2 Tablespoons	water
24	Popsicle sticks
	cake sprinkles (optional)

Preparation

1. Preheat oven to 350 degrees.
2. Combine cake mix, eggs and applesauce in a large bowl. Beat at medium speed for 4 minutes.

3. Line the muffin tins with cupcake papers and fill three-quarters full with batter. Put the cupcakes in the oven. Bake 17 to 20 minutes. Set aside to cool.

4. Unwrap the caramels and put them in a glass bowl with 2 tablespoons water. Put the bowl in the microwave and cook one minute at a time-stirring after each time. Do this until caramel is melted and is a good spreading consistency. Be very careful not to burn yourself on the warm caramel. Turn the cupcakes over and dip the tops in caramel sauce. (*Or* - just drizzle some caramel on top of the cupcakes with a spoon.) Insert a Popsicle stick in the middle of each cupcake and place on a platter. Add cake sprinkles if you like.

When you've finished making these treats, recite the charm so that they're complete.

Baker's Note
If you're using caramel sauce from a jar, heat the jar for 30-60 seconds in the microwave, and pour the sauce into a bowl. This will be runnier than the melted caramel candies.

October

It was Halloween afternoon, and the girls were sitting around the picnic table in Eva's backyard.

"I'm so excited for your class party tonight, Eva," said Daisy.

"I love that it's your birthday today, too," said Molly. "You're really lucky that you were born on such a fun holiday."

"I don't know," said Eva. "Halloween has always seemed so out of control to me."

"That's what I love most about it," said Daisy.

"Well," said Eva, "Thanks to Molly's gift, I'm much more excited about it this year." Eva turned to look at her friend. "It was so sweet of you to make me this haunted gingerbread house. I can't wait for everyone to see it tonight at the party."

Molly beamed.

"You're so creative," said Daisy. "It's really cool that everything on the house is edible."

The girls examined the haunted gingerbread house that was sitting in the middle of the picnic table.

Rock candy chimneys filled with cotton candy smoke dotted

the cookie-shingled roof. A porch with pretzel railings wrapped around the house, and a gingerbread cemetery stood behind it. Little cats, bats, witches, pumpkins, and ghosts were scattered all around the spooky gingerbread scene. Molly had made them out of a yummy, almond paste called marzipan, which she'd colored and sculpted into the various shapes.

"It's a masterpiece, Molly," said Daisy.

"Let's go inside and make some cupcakes for the party," said Eva. "I hope The Magic Cookbook shows up soon before my parents finish setting up the spook house in our barn. They've already been in there for hours."

"I can't wait to go through it tonight at the party. I'm sure it's going to be amazing," said Daisy.

When the girls and Ruffles walked into the kitchen, Eva gasped. The Magic Cookbook was flying around the room, cackling. Ruffles barked.

"Oh no," said Eva. "It's really scary."

"It's awesome," said Daisy.

"How did it get in here?" asked Molly.

"I don't know, but we need to catch it," said Eva, and she, Molly and Daisy joined Ruffles in chasing the cookbook around the kitchen.

"This is impossible," said Molly. "Every time we get close, it escapes."

"I wonder if it will ever come down," said Daisy, as she watched the cookbook circle overhead.

Eva sighed and sat down on a stool at the counter. "Oh, I give up."

No sooner were the words out of her mouth, than The Magic Cookbook stopped flapping its pages, and drifted down and landed right in front of Eva. It opened to a blank page, and the girls watched a recipe for Wild Witch Cupcakes appear.

"Thanks goodness," said Eva and read the magic cupcake charm aloud.

A witch's hat, a witch's broom,
Some mean cupcakes that likes to zoom,
These tasty morsels love the night,
And can give you quite a fright.

A witch's hat, a witch's broom,
Don't make them mad or they will fume,
And if you chase them, they will go
Faster than you'll ever know.

A witch's hat, a witch's broom,
Will stop flying round the room,
If you stay still the treats will land,
Very gently in your hands.

Eva and her friends mixed up the orange-flavored batter, added the milk chocolate chips, and poured it into the paper-lined muffin tins. After the cupcakes were baked and cooled, Eva coated them with chocolate frosting. Then an assortment of goodies appeared on the counter. Molly and Daisy made witches hats out of the chocolate kiss candies and chocolate wafers and put them on top of the cupcakes. Eva made tiny brooms out of the candy corns and toothpicks and stuck them through the cupcake sides.

Eva was very pleased. "They look like flying witches." She covered the large platter of cupcakes, making sure to tuck under the corners of the aluminum foil. *I don't want any air to get in,* she thought. *Or anything to get out.* Then Eva put the cupcakes on top of the refrigerator.

"Maybe they'll do something really wild at the party," said Daisy.

Eva bit her lip. "I just hope they don't get too out of control. I don't think I could handle it."

After the girls recited the cupcake charm, The Magic Cookbook flapped its pages once again and flew over to the corner fireplace and disappeared up the chimney.

"I bet that's how it got in here in the first place," said Daisy.

"Luckily you didn't have a fire going," said Molly.

Eva nodded and then glanced at the stove clock. "Let's go to my room and get our costumes on. Then we'll finish setting up."

An hour later, the moon was full and a cool breeze rustled through the remaining leaves on the trees. Mr. Perez lined the driveway with jack-o-lanterns and the straw scarecrows that he and his wife had made for the occasion. Mrs. Perez put trays of submarine sandwiches and popcorn balls next to the haunted gingerbread house on the picnic table outside.

Eva, Molly, and Daisy were dressed as vampires, and Ruffles pranced around wearing the little black cape that Daisy had made for him.

"The guests will arrive soon," said Eva. "Let's put the Wild Witch Cupcakes out with the other refreshments." She reached up to the top of the refrigerator and gasped. "Oh no!" The platter was empty except for the piece of aluminum foil that sat on top. It was shredded to bits.

"They must've flown right through that," said Daisy

"But where did they go?" asked Molly.

Eva looked suspiciously at Ruffles.

He whimpered and then slid between Daisy's legs.

Eva was about to lean over and smell his breath but stopped when she saw Daisy glaring at her.

"He didn't eat them," said Daisy. "But maybe he can follow their trail."

Ruffles put his snout in the air and sniffed. Then he lowered his head and sniffed the floor across the kitchen to the fireplace.

"Maybe they're hiding in the chimney," said Eva. She got down on her hands and knees and peered up the dark hole. A moment later, she pulled her head out. She coughed. "I can't see anything; it's too dark."

"What are we going to do?" Molly asked.

"I can't believe that we don't have cupcakes," said Eva. "My mom was going to make me a birthday cake, but I said that we had it covered."

There was a knock on the back kitchen door. Eva opened it and saw Hazel standing there with Velvet at her feet. Hazel was holding a cake that looked like a jack-o-lantern. It had orange frosting and a chocolate chip face.

"So good to see you girls this special Halloween evening," said Hazel. "And Eva, it's your birthday, too. How fine is that?"

"It's not that fine," Eva pouted. "Our cupcakes flew away."

Hazel just smiled and said, "I had a feeling that they might, so I made you this." She set the cake on the counter. "It's chocolate inside."

"Oh thank you. That's so sweet," said Eva. "But how did you know about the cupcakes?"

"Velvet told me," said Hazel.

Eva didn't know if this was a joke or not, but she giggled and then looked down at the cat who was winding his way through her legs, purring.

"Remember dear, things have a way of working themselves out if you let them." Then Hazel and Velvet slipped out the back door and set off into the night.

Thirty minutes later, the party was in full swing. Everyone was there except for Tiffany. Eva hoped that she wouldn't show up at all, but she had to admit that ever since the bake sale, Tiffany hadn't been quite so awful.

Eva's parents led everyone though the spook house. It was filled with rubber bats and toads, tattered mummies, big pumpkins, boney skeletons, and wooden pitchforks. White sheets hung from the rafters and looked like ghosts.

There was a table filled with bowls of revolting concoctions for the guests to stick their hands into. Hardboiled eggs had been soaking all day in a bowl of vinegar, and their shells had disintegrated. They were labeled, *Monster Eyeballs*. Strands of cold spaghetti covered with tomato sauce were, *Zombie Intestines*. Eva thought the most disgusting of all was the moldy bread that her father had poured warm water over. He called it, *Cow Mucus*.

A car horn blared from the end of the driveway. Everyone ran out of the barn just in time to see a limousine screech to a halt, causing a cloud of dust to rise. Mr. Perez rushed over and knocked on the driver's window. Eva didn't think he looked very commanding in his elf costume.

The driver got out. It was Jacques. Eva heard him apologize to her father. Then he opened the back door of the limousine, and Tiffany emerged. She was covered in fake tiger fur, had a long tail, and wore a fuzzy, striped cap with pointy ears.

"Sorry I'm late," said Tiffany. Then she joined Jessica Jones at the refreshment table, but Jessica turned and walked away.

I guess Jessica doesn't want to be her friend anymore, thought Eva.

Mrs. Perez was dressed in a flower fairy costume. After she passed out mugs of hot cider, she said to Eva, "Sweetheart, it looks like everything is running smoothly. Do you mind if your father and I go inside for just a few minutes?"

"Sure Mom, I've got everything under control."

After her parents left, Eva joined her classmates at the refreshment table where everyone was admiring Molly's haunted gingerbread house.

"Is there something inside of it?" asked Sasha Bell.

Eva looked closely. The melted candy stained-glass windows were glowing. Someone must've lit a candle inside the house, but who? Then Eva saw something—or someone—moving. Shivers ran down her spine. She looked at Molly and Daisy with wide eyes.

Suddenly, the front door of the haunted house blew open, and the pack of Wild Witch Cupcakes came flying out across the gingerbread porch and then into the gingerbread graveyard, knocking over tombstones along the way. The criminal cupcakes swooped over to the gingerbread porch, tore off the floorboards that Molly had made out of sticks of gum, and hauled them over to the back kitchen door. After stretching the gum between them, they taped the door shut with it. Then the cupcakes flew around Eva's house and did the same thing to every other door.

Oh no! My parents are trapped inside. But before Eva could free them, the band of cupcakes shot up into the sky, circled over the children like vultures, and then herded them into the barn, sliding the big door closed behind them. Then the cupcakes began dive-bombing the guests. Some children screamed, and others laughed.

"This is the best spook house ever," said Jake Farmer.

"I love it," yelled Josh Wiley.

"I hate it," screamed Tiffany.

"The cupcakes are much wilder than I thought they'd be," said Daisy.

"They're making a mess," said Eva.

"I wonder what they'll do next," said Molly.

The Wild Witch Cupcakes gathered together, propelled themselves upward to the loft, and pushed a pile of hay off. It came crashing down into the bowl of cow mucus, right next to where Eva was standing.

The cupcakes floated above, cackling. It was an eerie sound and everyone was silent until Jake Farmer yelled, "Let's catch 'em!"

There was total chaos, as children chased the cupcakes this way and that. Even Ruffles joined in the action. He was about to take a bite of a cupcake when it swatted him on the nose with its broom. He ran over to Daisy, his vampire cape trailing after him.

The cupcakes swarmed around Tiffany, fluttering their brooms and making a whirring sound.

Tiffany shrieked, "I don't like this one bit. Get me out of here!" She ran and crashed into a bale of hay in her way. Eva watched as six Wild Witch Cupcakes seized Tiffany by her tiger tail and carried her eight feet into the air. They would've taken her higher but Eva grabbed Tiffany's dangling arm, yanked her away from the vicious treats, and pulled her back down to the ground.

The cupcakes scattered and ducked under the hanging white sheets, lifting them up and off of the rafters. Eva thought that they looked just like real ghosts as they opened the barn door, and swooped through it. Everyone dashed outside after them.

"That was awesome," said Jake Farmer.

Tiffany burst into tears and looked at Eva. "Thank you for rescuing me." She ran to her waiting limo, flung herself into the back seat, and screamed, "Wake up, Jacques, and get me out of here. Now!"

The engine started, and the ghosts escorted the car to the end of the driveway, before it turned onto Main Street and headed back towards the Burnsley Mansion.

The Wild Witch Cupcakes flew out from under the sheets and up into a crow's nest near the top of the tallest tree at the end of the driveway. Eva noticed the silhouette of a cat sitting on a limb close by. *Is that Velvet?* she wondered.

"Let's get my parents," said Eva, racing towards the house. Molly, Daisy and Ruffles ran after her. As the girls began pulling the gum off the back door, Ruffles licked it faster and faster. A moment later, Eva's parents walked out.

"What on Earth has been going on out here?" asked Mr. Perez. "We've been trying to get out for ages, but the doors were all stuck."

Before the children could reply, Mrs. Perez chimed in, "Are you all okay?"

"Oh yes," said Eva. "Everything is under control." Then she, Daisy and Molly burst into fits of giggles.

Mr. Perez lit a campfire, and everyone gathered around and told ghost stories. Fifteen minutes later, Mrs. Perez stood up. "Stay right here, kids. We'll be right back."

"We promise." Mr. Perez winked and then went into the house with his wife.

Eva heard a swishing sound above her. "What's that noise?" she whispered loud enough for everyone to hear.

The children looked up and saw the Wild Witch Cupcakes overhead, fluttering their brooms. Everyone froze. The cupcakes drifted down, landed in the children's hands and were devoured before they could escape again.

A minute later, Eva's parents walked out singing *"Happy Birthday,"* and carrying the jack-o-lantern cake from Hazel. "I hope you're all hungry," said Mrs. Perez.

After Eva blew out the eleven birthday candles, she smiled and looked down at her vampire costume. She was completely covered in cow mucus. *Too bad Dexter and Arlo aren't here to make it disappear with one of their magic tricks.* Eva giggled. *Oh well, maybe it's okay for things to get a little messy and out control once in a while.*

Maybe.

Wild Witch Cupcakes

Magic Cupcake Charm
A witch's hat, a witch's broom,
Some mean cupcakes that likes to zoom,
These tasty morsels love the night,
And can give you quite a fright.

A witch's hat, a witch's broom,
Don't make them mad or they will fume,
And if you chase them, they will go
Faster than you'll ever know.

A witch's hat, a witch's broom,
Will stop flying round the room,
If you stay still the treats will land,
Very gently in your hands.

Ingredients for 24 Cupcakes

1 (18.25 ounce) package	yellow cake mix
1 (3 ounce) package	instant vanilla pudding mix
1 cup	buttermilk
3/4 cup	vegetable oil
1/2 cup	water
4	eggs
1 cup	semisweet chocolate chips
1 teaspoon	orange extract
24	cupcake papers

Topping

48	toothpicks
24	round chocolate wafer cookies
24	chocolate kiss candies
24	candy corns
1 (16 ounce) tub	white frosting
	red and yellow food coloring (to make orange)

Preparation

1. Preheat oven to 350 degrees.
2. Combine the cake and pudding mixes, buttermilk, oil, orange extract, water, and eggs in a large bowl. Beat at medium speed for 4 minutes. Stir in the chocolate chips.
3. Line the muffin tins with cupcake papers and fill three-quarters full with batter. Put the cupcakes in the oven and bake for 17 to 20 minutes. Set aside to cool.
4. Dye the frosting orange— add red and yellow food coloring one drop at a time until you get the desired shade. Then frost the cupcakes. To make a witch's hat, put a dab of frosting on the bottom of a chocolate kiss candy and stick it on a chocolate wafer. Let a little bit of the frosting show so that it looks like a ribbon around the hat. To make a broom, gently insert the end of a toothpick into the tip of a candy corn. Put hats on top of the

cupcakes, and slip brooms through the sides. Slip an additional toothpick into the opposite side of each cupcake so that it looks like the broomsticks go all the way through.

When you've finished making these treats, recite the charm so that they're complete.

November

Mr. Clark stood at the front of the classroom. "As you all know, the school holiday fair is coming up next month."

Eva cheered louder than any of the other fifth graders. The big event was almost here.

Mr. Clark continued, "In the past, Mr. Vine always chose a fifth grader to be in charge of organizing the fair. He picked a student who could handle the hard work and who was always well-prepared."

Eva beamed. She knew that Mr. Clark was describing *her*. She couldn't wait to pick the theme for the fair, the decorations, the types of food that would be served, the games that everyone would play, the design for the posters and invitations, and the songs that the musicians would perform.

Eva was positive that Mr. Clark was about to announce her name at any moment. She was going to organize the holiday fair!

"Well, we're going to do things a bit differently this year," said Mr. Clark. "I'm adding a twist."

Eva gulped. *Oh no!*

"Now bear with me as I explain," said Mr. Clark. "Since Thanksgiving is this month, I'd like for our class to bake desserts for charity. And to make it more interesting I'm turning it into a contest."

Eva was on the edge of her seat. What did this have to do with the holiday fair? Beads of sweat were forming on her forehead. What was he going to say next?

Mr. Clark smiled at his students. "Choose a friend or two to work with. The team that bakes the most desserts will be in charge of the holiday fair that will be held at Blake's Rare Books this year."

"Eva, your face is green. Are you okay?" whispered Molly.

Eva was too stunned to reply.

Tiffany raised her hand. "If we don't have any friends, is it okay if we work by ourselves?"

"Well Tiffany, I'm sure that you have friends," said Mr. Clark. "But if you'd rather work alone, that's fine. That way if you win the contest, you'll be the only one in charge of the fair."

Eva's ears perked up. *At least that's one piece of good news. Of course, I want to be the only one in charge of the fair. And, of course, I want to use The Magic Cookbook to make cupcakes for the contest, so that I'm sure to win.* Then she bit her lip. *But how am I going to tell Molly and Daisy that I don't want their help this month? I don't want to end up like Tiffany and not have any friends.*

* * *

The Sunday before Thanksgiving, Eva was sitting in her kitchen drinking hot chocolate and waiting for The Magic Cookbook to show up. Her parents were next door in their shop.

When the doorbell rang, Eva ran to answer it. Maybe it was the cookbook. But when she opened the door, she saw Molly, Daisy, and Ruffles standing there. Before Eva could stop them they walked into the kitchen.

"We couldn't wait any longer for you to invite us over to make cupcakes," said Daisy.

"We knew you probably just forgot," said Molly.

Ruffles wandered over to his favorite spot under the kitchen table and fell asleep.

"Oh sorry," Eva mumbled. "The Magic Cookbook still hasn't arrived, so I don't think it's coming this month. It's probably best if you all go home, and bake something for the contest alone."

"Are you trying to get rid of us before the cookbook gets here?" asked Daisy.

Eva's face flushed. "Of course not."

"Yes, you are," said Daisy. "You're trying to get rid of us so that you can win the contest by yourself and be the only one to organize the holiday fair. You're not being very nice, Eva."

Eva wasn't sure what to say. "Well, um, a…"

The front doorbell rang again. *What if The Magic Cookbook is at the door this time?* She reluctantly went to answer it. A moment later, Eva returned to the kitchen with her hands behind her. She was holding something.

"What's behind your back?" asked Molly.

"Oh, nothing," said Eva.

"Come on, Eva," said Daisy. "You're hiding something from us. What is it?"

Eva's face felt hot as she brought a large mailing envelope out from behind her and set it on the counter. "It's just this," she said. "Someone left this on the doormat."

"Your name is written on it," said Molly, adjusting her glasses and staring at the package. "It might be The Magic Cookbook. You've got to open it now so we can see."

"I don't want to bore you," said Eva. "I'll open it after you leave."

But suddenly the package started to shake. Then it doubled in size, then shrank to the size of a cupcake, and then returned to normal. Then the envelope popped opened, and The Magic Cookbook slid out.

"You can't get rid of us now," said Daisy. "We're staying!"

Eva shrugged, "Well okay. But when we win the contest, I get to be the head organizer of the party, and you can be my helpers."

"Okay, we'll be your helpers," said Molly.

"But not your slaves, right?" said Daisy.

"Right," said Eva, just as the cookbook flipped open to a blank page, and a recipe for Pumpkin Pie Cupcakes appeared.

Daisy's face lit up. "I'm crazy about pumpkin."

"Me too," said Molly. "When I'm around pumpkin desserts, I can't control myself. It gets bad."

Eva knew that this was true. Her friends both loved pumpkin. Last Thanksgiving at The Honeysuckle Inn's feast, Eva watched them eat an entire pumpkin pie between them. And they would have eaten a second one if Daisy's mom hadn't stepped in. "Save some for everyone else. You'll get sick," Mrs. Humphrey had warned.

Eva rolled her eyes at the memory and wondered, *how can anyone lose control like that?* Then she read the magic cupcake charm.

Little pies, little pies,
Watch them grow before your eyes,
Taste so good they're like a dream,
Top them off with sweet whipped cream,
Little pies, little pies,
Watch them grow before your eyes!

Giant pies, giant pies,
All aboard for your surprise,
You'll go fast so hold on tight,
Look around—it's quite a sight,
Giant pies, giant pies,
All aboard for your surprise!

"This is so exciting," said Molly.

The girls whipped up the pumpkin batter and poured it into the miniature graham cracker crusts that had appeared. Then they baked the twenty-four cupcakes and let them cool next to The Magic Cookbook, still sitting on the counter.

After they recited the magic cupcake charm, Eva bit her lip. "They're cute, but I wonder if they're too small for me to win the contest."

"Don't you mean for *us* to win the contest?" asked Daisy.

"Oh yeah. I meant us," Eva replied.

Molly interrupted. "I'm really sorry, Eva, but I can't control myself any longer." She grabbed a cupcake and took a bite. "Yum."

Immediately, Daisy did the same. "Double yum," she exclaimed.

Ruffles woke up from his nap and pranced over. Daisy handed him a taste.

Eva's eyes widened. "I can't believe you guys. Now we only have twenty-two cupcakes left. What if it's not enough to win the contest?"

"We'll still win," said Daisy.

Molly nodded. "Don't worry Eva. It will all work out."

Eva's friends kept eating until, *POP, POP*, the cupcakes in their hands grew into full-sized pumpkin pies.

"Woo-hoo!" Daisy and Molly shouted.

"Woof-hoo!" Ruffles barked.

POP, POP, POP! The girls looked at the rest of the cupcakes on the counter. They were all growing.

"How wonderful," said Eva, "They're not little anymore."

"This is the best day of my life," said Daisy, eyeing the pies.

"Eva, you've got to try one," said Molly. "You'll love it."

Eva shook her head and then watched in disgust as her friends finished off the pies in their hands. "You guys are going to get sick."

Eva began covering the pies on the counter with foil and whisking them away to the kitchen pantry.

"There are still twenty-two left," said Daisy. "That's way more than we need to win."

"You're just saying that because you want to eat more," said Eva, picking up another pie and preparing to cover it.

As if The Magic Cookbook couldn't stand another moment of their bickering, it leaped off the counter, scurried out of the kitchen and down the hall, and shoved open the front door. With a pie still in her hands, Eva dashed out to the front porch with Molly, Daisy, and Ruffles close behind her. They arrived just in time to see The Magic Cookbook leap over the porch railing and run away down the driveway.

"I don't really blame it for leaving," said Molly. "We were being really annoying."

"I sure hope it comes back for my final turn next month," said Eva, right before she heard loud honking and flapping sounds above her. The girls looked up into the sky and saw hundreds of Canada geese flying overhead.

"They must be flying south for the . . . " Eva gasped, as the pie in her hands began to grow, and grow, and grow. When she couldn't hold it any longer, she let go. The pie hovered in midair, and then grew, and grew some more. Then the pie bumped into Eva's knees and she fell on top of it. She expected to sink right in, but since it had a cake filling rather than custard, Eva stayed on top of the firm, cushiony surface. She felt like she was on a big bed.

Eva looked over at Molly and Daisy who were climbing onto the other side of the floating pie. Ruffles leaped up and joined them. Daisy put an arm around him, and he licked her face. Then he licked the giant pie beneath them.

When the geese honked again, the giant pie rose above the porch, waited for a moment and then took off, just like a magic carpet.

"Yippee," yelled Daisy as the pie shot above Eva's house.

As they flew higher and higher, Eva yelled, "Hold on tight."

She jammed her feet into the pie and grabbed tightly onto the rim of the graham cracker crust surrounding them. Then she peered over the edge and looked at the shrinking houses and trees below. Her long hair whipped behind her, and she actually started to enjoy herself. "I can't believe this is happening," she said.

"We're in a pie in the sky." Molly laughed.

The pie quickly caught up with the flock of geese, where it zoomed into the lead at the very head of the V-formation.

The girls soon learned that they could actually steer the pie by leaning one way or the other — like riding a sled. They also found that when they veered any direction that the geese behind them would follow. It was exhilarating.

Eva pointed at the town of Willow Brook below. There was The Honeysuckle Inn, there was Blake's Rare Books, and she could just make out something galloping along the sidewalk.

"It's The Magic Cookbook," yelled Eva as she watched the book speed up a hill to the brick mansion that sat on top. It was Tiffany's house.

As Eva and her friends leaned back in their pie, they slowed down, and a big gray goose skirted around them and flew forward. He honked at them and then took the lead.

The girls aimed their pie downward, broke away from the flock and descended towards Tiffany's house. Maybe they could catch The Magic Cookbook. But as they got closer, they saw it throw itself against the Burnsleys' front door. A moment later, Tiffany came out. Eva gulped as she watched Tiffany pick the book up, carry it inside, and shut the door behind her.

Minutes later, Eva and her friends landed back on her family's front porch. They sat in silence for a moment, and then the pie suddenly vanished into the cool, autumn air.

"I'm really confused," said Eva as she caught her breath. "Why did the cookbook go over to Tiffany's?"

"Maybe it's trying to punish us for arguing," said Molly as she straightened her windblown braids.

"Let's talk about it while we eat another pie," suggested Daisy, her short blond curls tangled from their recent flight.

"No," said Eva firmly. "This is the last time I'll say it. You cannot eat any more pies. We only have twenty-one left now, and I want to win the contest!"

When the girls walked into the kitchen, they found Eva's mom sitting at the counter. "I was wondering where you all were. I've been admiring your pies in the pantry. Maybe I should hire you to help me arrange flowers. I can see that you're very hard workers." Mrs. Perez smiled and stood up. "I'll be in my office if you need me." She kissed her daughter on the cheek, and Eva watched her walk out of the room and down the hall.

When Eva turned back towards the kitchen, her friends were gone. Maybe they went out the back kitchen door while she wasn't looking? Eva heard rustling sounds in the dried leaves outside. She ran to the window and saw Daisy and Molly running down the driveway in their big, winter coats. Ruffles chased after them.

*　*　*

The next morning, Eva was loading the pies into her mom's car. They were going to drive them over to school where Mr. Clark would count and deliver them to charities in the area. He would announce the contest winners after the Thanksgiving break.

"Seventeen, eighteen, nineteen." Eva loaded the last of the pies. Maybe she'd miscounted, but when she counted again, there were still just nineteen.

Eva ran back into the house and then into the kitchen pantry. The two missing pies were nowhere to be seen. Had Daisy and Molly each smuggled a pie out with them yesterday? Is that why they left so fast?

Eva called Daisy on the telephone. She should've been here by now to help.

Mrs. Humphrey answered. "Oh, hello, Eva. I was just about to call you. Daisy is sick in bed with a stomachache and won't be able to come over. I caught her finishing off a whole pumpkin pie in her room last night. She'll probably be in bed for a while. I'm afraid she might even miss our wonderful Thanksgiving feast here at the inn."

When Eva called Molly, she got a very similar story from Mrs. McGregor.

Eva was mad. So mad in fact, that she was actually glad that her two best friends had stomachaches.

It serves them right. Eva frowned. *Because of them, I might not win the contest.*

Pumpkin Pie Cupcakes

Magic Cupcake Charm

Little pies, little pies,
Watch them grow before your eyes,
Taste so good they're like a dream,
Top them off with sweet whipped cream,
Little pies, little pies,
Watch them grow before your eyes!

Giant pies, giant pies,
All aboard for your surprise,
You'll go fast so hold on tight,
Look around—it's quite a sight,
Giant pies, giant pies,
All aboard for your surprise!

Ingredients for 24 Cupcakes

1 (18.25 ounce) package	yellow cake mix
1/2 teaspoon	ground cinnamon
1/4 teaspoon	ground nutmeg
1 & 1/4 cup	half & half cream
2 tablespoons	vegetable oil
3	eggs
3/4 cup	canned pumpkin
24	miniature graham cracker piecrusts (*or* 1 box of graham crackers and 24 cupcake papers)

Topping

1 can	whipped cream

Preparation

1. Preheat oven to 350 degrees.
2. Combine the cake mix, cinnamon, and nutmeg in a large bowl. Add the cream, oil, and eggs. Beat at medium speed for 4 minutes. Add the pumpkin and mix until well blended.
3. Spoon the filling into the mini graham cracker piecrusts (or crush the graham crackers with a rolling pin and sprinkle them into the bottoms of the cupcake papers). They should be about two-thirds full. Put the cupcakes in the oven. Bake 15 minutes or until done. Set aside to cool.
4. Serve the Pumpkin Pie Cupcakes with whipped cream.

When you've finished making these treats, recite the charm so that they're complete.

December

The first day back from Thanksgiving break, Mr. Clark said to his class, "The contest was a huge success. You all made wonderful desserts, and the charities that received them were very grateful. Now, the news you've all been waiting for."

Eva held her breath and crossed her fingers.

"Tiffany made twenty-three pies and is our winner, so she will organize the holiday fair."

Tiffany let out a little squeal and clapped her hands. "Yay!"

Mr. Clark smiled at Tiffany. "Very impressive, my dear, especially since you baked the desserts all by yourself. I certainly wasn't expecting anyone to make that many." Mr. Clark turned to Eva, Molly and Daisy. "And your team came in second with nineteen pies. Wonderful work."

Eva refused to look over at her friends. She hadn't talked to either of them over the Thanksgiving break, and she certainly wasn't going to talk to them now.

Tiffany raised her hand.

"Yes, Tiffany?" said Mr. Clark.

"I just want to tell everyone what happened the other day," said Tiffany. "Someone was banging on our front door, and when I went to answer it, I found a book sitting on the welcome mat. I brought it into the house and it actually flipped open to a blank page. A second later a recipe appeared. It was all very magical."

Jake Farmer and his buddies snickered, and Eva could hear Daisy and Molly gasp, but she still wouldn't look at them.

"Hmm." Mr. Clark scratched his head. "That's very interesting, Tiffany. Maybe you can share the recipe with us."

"I would if I could," Tiffany replied. "But after I made the desserts, the cookbook just disappeared. I've looked everywhere, but it's gone."

"Well, I hope you find it. You're a very good baker," said Mr. Clark.

"No, I'm not," said Tiffany to her shocked classmates. "This is the first thing I've ever baked. Normally Jacques does it all for me, and I take all the credit, but he's on vacation in Paris."

Mr. Clark looked uneasy. "But you are still very creative, my dear. That sand castle you made last summer was astonishing."

"Oh, I didn't make that either," said Tiffany. "I think that Daisy did, but I can't figure out how."

Everyone was silent. What had gotten into Tiffany? It was true that ever since her mouth got stuck at the bake sale she'd been telling fewer lies. But this was different. She actually seemed nice.

"Don't you want to hear about my ride on a giant flying pie?" Tiffany asked Mr. Clark.

"Um, no Tiffany. I think we'll skip that for now," replied Mr. Clark.

Eva was dying to talk to her friends, but she just couldn't. Not yet anyway. After all, she would've won first place if Daisy and Molly hadn't made such pigs of themselves.

Then Eva bit her lip. *I wonder if The Magic Cookbook will come back to my house for the final month or if it will go over to Tiffany's instead.* It was all very worrisome.

After lunch, Mr. Clark announced that Tiffany had chosen a gingerbread theme for the holiday party.

Eva had to admit that it was a great idea. She couldn't help thinking that she should have been the one to come up with it.

"And," said Mr. Clark, "Tiffany has some other news to tell you."

Eva watched Tiffany walk to the front of the class.

"Well," she said. "I've decided that I need your help organizing the holiday party. It's just too much for me to do on my own, and I thought it would be more fun this way."

Eva couldn't believe her ears. "What?" she accidentally blurted out.

Tiffany spoke again. "I said, I've decided that I need everyone's help organizing the holiday party. So, please sign up for the committee you'd like to be on. Let's get started right away so we can have the best holiday fair ever."

The kids were all speechless. What had happened to Tiffany? Eva wondered if an alien had taken over her body—a really nice alien.

After another minute of silence, Mr. Clark said, "Thank you, Tiffany. You've reminded us that great leaders always ask for assistance."

Eva felt like going home and crawling under her covers. But instead, she signed up to be on the refreshment committee with Beth Summers and Amy Lin. They decided to ask everyone in the class to bring their favorite gingerbread treats that would be served with delicious hot cocoa and spiced cider.

Eva hoped that The Magic Cookbook would return to her house with a recipe for gingerbread cupcakes. *And I'll bake them by myself this time,* thought Eva. *Which is what I should've done last month. At least I can get excited about that.*

But as the days passed, Eva grew less and less excited, and more and more miserable. She realized that she wasn't even angry at Molly and Daisy anymore. She just felt sad and lonely, and she began to wonder if she'd handled everything badly. *Maybe I should've tried a pumpkin cupcake. Maybe it was okay that Daisy and Molly lost control. Maybe I should learn to relax and stop telling everyone what to do all the time.* Then Eva remembered what Hazel had told her last month. *Things have a way of working themselves out if you let them.*

At school Eva noticed that even though many of the fifth graders were warming up to Tiffany, she was usually alone. It looked as if Jessica had moved on and made other friends. *Just like Daisy and Molly,* thought Eva.

Daisy and Molly were on the decorating team with Sasha Bell and seemed to be having a wonderful time. Eva overheard them talking one day.

"How about if you two come over to my place on Saturday, and we'll make gingerbread ornaments for the tree?" asked Daisy.

"Oh, that sounds like so much fun. I can't wait," replied Sasha.

"You'll meet Ruffles too," said Molly. "You're going to love him."

Eva felt like she'd been replaced, and it felt awful.

* * *

The day before the holiday party, Eva was moping around the kitchen. The cookbook was nowhere to be seen. *I guess I won't be able to bake that final batch of cupcakes after all. Obviously, The Magic Cookbook has gone over to Tiffany's house instead.*

There was a knock on the back kitchen door and Eva ran to answer it. Maybe it was the cookbook. Eva pulled the door open and saw Hazel standing there.

"Hello, dear. Your mother tells me that you still aren't speaking to Daisy and Molly? I wanted to see how you were doing."

A tear rolled down Eva's cheek. She sighed. "I've been better. I just wish I hadn't been so bossy. I've ruined everything."

Hazel patted her on the back. "I'm sure you can make it right again."

"But what if Molly and Daisy don't want to be my friend anymore?" asked Eva.

"Well," said Hazel, "I doubt if that's the case, but maybe The Magic Cookbook can help you?"

"I don't think it's coming back," said Eva.

"Oh yes it is." Hazel smiled and then opened her shoulder bag. The Magic Cookbook leaped out and landed in Eva's arms. A red satin ribbon was tied around it.

"Oh, thank you!" Eva gave Hazel a big hug and then asked, "By the way, where's Velvet? He's usually with you."

"He's around here somewhere. I'm sure he'll show up soon," said Hazel, as she walked away.

Eva set the book on the kitchen counter. When she untied the satin ribbon, the book fell open to a blank page, and a recipe for Gift Wrapped Cupcakes appeared. It was written in flashing red and green ink.

Gift-wrapped cupcakes—what's inside?
You'll find out, when they're untied.
What's the gift you're wishing for?
A new toy or something more?
When you look your gift will be
Underneath the Christmas tree.

As Eva read through the charm a couple of times, she wondered what gift *she* was wishing for.

Eva mixed up a batch of the gingerbread cupcakes and decorated them with green frosting, candy canes and cake sprinkles. Next, she tied red licorice bows and set them on top of the cupcakes.

Eva waited for the cookbook to snap shut and disappear or fly out the door or something. It didn't budge. *Hmm*, she thought. *Maybe I'm supposed to make more. It would be nice to make enough so that everyone can have one, and lots of people will be at the fair.* Instantly, more ingredients appeared on the countertop.

Two hours and four batches of cupcakes later, Eva was exhausted, and the kitchen was a huge mess. She had baked over 100 cupcakes. She looked at The Magic Cookbook and asked, "Can we stop now? Please?"

The book closed and jumped down to the floor. Then it circled through Eva's legs, causing green and red sparks to fly.

Eva leaned over and patted the book. "Thank you for everything. You're a wonderful friend, and friends are more important than winning a silly contest."

After the book disappeared, Eva smiled. She knew exactly what she'd wish for when she bit into a Gift-Wrapped Cupcake at the party.

* * *

At the holiday fair the next night, Eva walked over to the large refreshment table with her parents and put a basket of gingerbread cupcakes at each end. She attached a copy of the magic cupcake charm to each of the basket handles.

> Gift-wrapped cupcakes—what's inside?
> You'll find out, when they're untied.
> What's the gift you're wishing for?
> A new toy or something more?
> When you look your gift will be
> Underneath the Christmas tree.

Eva gazed around Blake's Rare Books. The fifth graders had decked it out for the occasion, and it looked like the inside of a giant gingerbread house. Life-sized gingerbread men cut out of brown paper lined the walls, and paper-mache candy canes framed the doors. The windows were decorated to look like stained glass. Tables were covered with red cloths, and boughs of holly were scattered everywhere. Red and green candles twinkled around the room, smelling of cinnamon and pine.

A beautiful evergreen tree glistened at one end of the room. The decorating committee had decorated it with tiny white lights, red glass balls, candy canes, gingerbread ornaments, and strands of cranberries and popcorn. A band played lively holiday music in the adjoining room, and a big fire crackled in the fireplace. Ruffles slept next to it, snoring.

A sprig of mistletoe hung over Velvet's window-seat cushion and Arlo, Dexter and some of the other younger children took turns trying to kiss the gray cat. When he'd had enough, Velvet jumped down from his cushion and dashed behind some bookshelves.

Mr. Clark rang a little bell. "Welcome to our holiday fair.

Thank you for coming. Please help yourselves to the wonderful gingerbread treats provided by our fifth graders."

Everyone clapped and then made a beeline for the tempting piles of gingerbread cookies, cakes and puddings. Most people carried their refreshments into the next room where they could dance and play games.

Eva stayed at the refreshment table and reached into one of the baskets for a Gifted-Wrapped Cupcake. Then she noticed that Daisy and Molly had each just taken one as well from the basket at the other end of the table.

She thought to herself, *I wish that Daisy and Molly were my friends again.* Quickly adding, *but only if they want to be friends with me, too.* She untied the licorice bow on top of the cupcake and closed her eyes.

Instantly, she felt something scratchy rubbing against her face. She opened her eyes. What was she doing under the Christmas tree? She heard laughter next to her. Daisy and Molly were under the tree as well. They all wiggled out.

As the girls stood up, Daisy and Molly asked Eva, "Did you wish for us, too?"

Eva nodded.

"We knew that those had to be magic cupcakes, and the only wish either of us had was to have you back as our friend," said Daisy.

"But only if you wanted to be friends with us," Molly chimed in, pulling a pine needle out of her hair and adjusting her glasses.

Eva didn't know whether to laugh or cry. "I made the exact same wish." She hugged her friends. "You guys are the best present ever!"

The three girls hurried back to the refreshment table just in time to see Tiffany and Jessica untie the bows on their cupcakes and then disappear. A second later, Eva and her friends spotted them under the tree.

Tiffany and Jessica crawled out, laughed, and hugged.

"I've missed you so much. Having you back as my friend is the best gift I've ever gotten. I'm really sorry if I was ever mean to you," Tiffany said to Jessica.

I guess we're not that different after all, thought Eva.

Then Molly and Daisy led Eva around the Christmas tree, showing her their handmade gingerbread ornaments.

"Here's the first one we made." Daisy pointed to a gingerbread snowflake covered with sparkly, white sugar.

"This was the second one." Molly walked a few steps and showed Eva a red, frosted heart.

"This rainbow was the third and the fourth was this paintbrush," Daisy added.

Eva's eyes lit up. "That's brilliant. You made a gingerbread ornament for every month of magic cupcakes." Eva continued walking around the tree. There was a golf club, a puppy that looked like Ruffles, a campfire, a sandcastle, a caramel apple, a witch, and a pumpkin pie with a big bite taken out of it.

"We didn't know what to make for December," said Molly.

For the next half hour the girls watched other guests untie the licorice bows on top of the gift-wrapped cupcakes and then find their gifts under the Christmas tree.

Mrs. McGregor got a new set of cookware for her catering business, Mr. McGregor got a book about changing weather patterns, Mrs. Humphrey got five silk pillows for her sofa, and Eva's parents got a new computer with software to help them organize their business.

Mrs. Perez gave her daughter a hug. "This is wonderful. It means that we won't have to work as hard, and we can be at home more with you."

Eva beamed.

The girls' parents all turned to Hazel. "Who are these presents from?"

"Santa Claus, of course," replied Hazel. Then they watched Arlo and Dexter untie their cupcake bows and rush to look under the tree for their gifts. They each got magic sets.

"Awesome!" said Arlo. "I can't wait to learn more tricks."

"Me, too," said Dexter, and the boys ran to an empty couch across the room to get started.

After their parents drifted back to the dance floor, Eva, Daisy, and Molly watched Hazel untie the bow on her cupcake and then pick out a shiny package under the tree.

"What did you wish for?" Eva asked.

Hazel's eyes sparkled as she removed the silver wrapping paper. There was The Magic Cookbook, and it was glowing. Hazel beckoned the girls over to the fireplace, where Ruffles was alone and still napping.

"Its time for you to say goodbye," said Hazel as she held up the cookbook.

Molly leaned over and said in her calm, sweet voice, "I'm going to miss you, but I know that we'll always be friends. Thank you for helping me to believe in myself and in my artistic gifts. I'll never forget you."

"Thank you so much for helping me become more responsible," said Daisy. She stroked the book's cover, and it snuggled up to her. "But mostly, thank you for helping me find Ruffles."

When Ruffles heard his name, he woke up and licked the cookbook with his long tongue. The book quivered.

"Even though it was a bit messy at times, it's been the best year ever," said Eva. "Thank you for helping me to relax and for showing me what's most important." She smiled at Daisy and Molly, and they smiled back.

Then The Magic Cookbook flipped open to a blank page. A moment later a poem emerged.

> The year is now up—your lessons are done,
> It's been a great ride, we've had lots of fun,
> Our lives are better than they were before
> We found each other at this rare bookstore.

The girls clapped.

"And by the way," Eva said to the cookbook. "Did you do something to Tiffany?"

The cookbook flipped open to the last page of the book and revealed its final poem.

> How do you make Tiffany sweet?
> Give her something good to eat.
> When will she start being nice?
> When she smells some pumpkin spice.
> Will she always stay this way?
> That's her choice—it's hard to say.

When Eva, Daisy, Molly, and Hazel finally stopped laughing, The Magic Cookbook snapped shut. The girls and Ruffles followed Hazel through some aisles of books to a quiet spot. They watched the cookbook spring out of Hazel's hands and land back up on the same shelf where the girls had first come across it.

Ten minutes later all of the guests gathered together around the Christmas tree. Eva stood up on a chair and said, "Let's give

Hazel Blake a round of applause for hosting the holiday party and for everything else that she does for us."

Everyone clapped and cheered.

"And let's give another round of applause for Tiffany Burnsley. She's the best holiday fair organizer ever."

As everyone cheered even louder, Tiffany looked over at Eva, Molly, and Daisy, and smiled.

* * *

Just before she left the party, Molly handed Hazel a small, painted plaque. "Will you please give this to Velvet? I made it especially for him."

Hazel kissed Molly on the cheek. "That's so sweet of you, my dear. I'll hang it next to his bed right now, so he can see it when he shows up again. I'm sure he will love it."

After the last guests left, Hazel walked back to the shelf where The Magic Cookbook was still sitting. She called up to it, "You can come out now."

As the cookbook leaped down to the floor, it transformed into the soft gray cat with green eyes. Velvet.

For a moment his eyes met Hazel's. Then Velvet sauntered over to his window seat cushion, gazed at the plaque on the wall from Molly, and purred.

> Soft and gray with emerald eyes,
> Full of mystery and surprise,
> Sneaks away to new frontiers,
> But each time he reappears,
> He can always smell a rat,
> Velvet is the purr-fect cat.

Gift Wrapped Cupcakes

Magic Cupcake Charm
Gift-wrapped cupcakes—what's inside?
You'll find out, when they're untied.
What's the gift you're wishing for?
A new toy or something more?
When you look your gift will be
Underneath the Christmas tree.

Ingredients for 24 Cupcakes

2 (14.5 ounce) packages	gingerbread cake mix
2 & 1/2 cups	eggnog or whole milk
2	eggs
1 (16 ounce) can	pear halves (drained)
24	cupcake papers

Topping

24	small candy canes
	green food coloring
1 (16 ounce) tub	vanilla frosting
	cake sprinkles
	red shoestring licorice

Preparation

1. Preheat oven to 350 degrees.
2. Chop up the pears and combine them with the cake mix, eggnog, and eggs in a large bowl. Beat at medium speed for 4 minutes.
3. Line the muffin tins with cupcake papers and fill three-quarters full. Put the cupcakes in the oven. Bake 15 minutes or until done. Set aside to cool.

4. Color the frosting green and frost the cupcakes. Cut licorice into 4 to 5-inch pieces and tie into bows. Put a licorice bow on each cupcake and add a candy cane. Sprinkle the tops with colored sprinkles.
5. Make additional cupcakes if you have leftover batter.

When you've finished making these treats, recite the charm so that they're complete.